Date Due

SEP 17 '99	OCT 05 '00		
OCT 14 '00	OCT 13 '00		
OCT 30 '99	JUL 27 '01		
NOV 10 '99			
DEC 23 '99	FEB 06 '04		
DEC 29 '99	MAR 10 '06		
JAN 04 '06	DEC 15 2015		
FEB 02 '00	NOV 08 2015		
MAR 17 '00		9103	3 0 AON
2.7	'02 0 0 NOV		
AUG 17 '00			

Dreadful Lies

Dreadful Lies

Michèle Bailey

St. Martin's Press ☆ New York

A THOMAS DUNNE BOOK.
An imprint of St. Martin's Press.

Library of Congress Cataloging-in-Publication Data

Bailey, Michèle.
    Dreadful lies / Michèle Bailey.
       p.   cm.
    "A Thomas Dunne book."
    ISBN 0-312-14323-0
    I. Title.
  PR6052.A3188D74   1996
  823'.914—dc20   96-5200
                                                   CIP

First published in Great Britain by Macmillan London Limited,
a division of Pan Macmillan Publishers Limited

First U.S. Edition: July 1996

10 9 8 7 6 5 4 3 2 1

Dreadful Lies

Chapter 1

Have you ever spent three days photocopying?

Neither had I, and I never want to again. But work is work and we've all got to eat.

The temp agency needed two English language secretaries with 150 w.p.m. shorthand to take verbatim notes of a legal enquiry for a well-known Brussels law firm. Ever so exciting, said the agency lady, looking at us hopefully over her half-moon glasses, and the rates are terribly good.

Hadn't they heard of tape recorders, thought I, but who am I to argue, especially at those rates? And I used to be able to get up to 150 w.p.m. far back in prehistoric times. But the assignment fell through at the last minute, as plum assignments are apt to do, and rather than have no work at all, we took what we could get, Ann Wilcox and I, and that's how we ended up in one of Brussels' most prestigious office blocks on the Avenue de Tervuren, photocopying.

You get to learn a lot about photocopiers in three days. They break down every five minutes, for a start. I'm only surprised the manufacturers don't give a technician away free with every machine. We got to know ours very well. He was a morose little man from Verviers, a depressed town in Wallonia. He blamed the economic situation on the immigrants, combined with unfair competition from the Flemish. The French-speaking Walloons think the Flemish are a bunch of jumped-up peasants. The Flemish think the Walloons are work-shy whiners. I don't get involved in national disputes, so I shook my head and

1

said what could you expect with forty new governments since the last war?

Like most prestigious office blocks, this one was only prestigious in the parts the public gets to see. From the outside, it looked like a stack of space-age egg-boxes, all fancy moulding and shiny glass. Inside, it was cramped and rather shabby. I don't know what you had to do to qualify for an office with a window. Most people made do with rabbit-hutches made out of buff-coloured partitions. Ann and I didn't even have that. The photocopiers were in a sort of cupboard in the corridor. Ventilation was nil.

The office was a European headquarters and we were photocopying budgets: all highly confidential material, for anyone who cared. Every so often, a highly coiffured lady with spectacles on chains round her neck popped her head in to make sure we weren't microfilming for the competition. It got very hot after an hour or two. It was early summer and the weather was uncharacteristically warm. I asked if we could bring in swimsuits, but the suggestion was not well received. Then I put a sign up saying 'Sauna', but a rather frosty young English executive came by and asked if I wouldn't mind taking it down again. I asked how he would feel about working under these conditions and said it was a good thing neither Ann nor I was pregnant. He gave me a cautious look and retired, taking the sign with him. I thought of putting another one up, but what the hell! We were only there for three days.

Half an hour later, the executive was back. He needed a photocopy made. Men make a great thing about being able to strip down an engine in five minutes flat, but most of them are totally helpless when faced with a photocopier. That, I suppose, is why they have secretaries.

I interrupted the programme and made his copy. He smiled. He was an OK-looking young man.

He said: 'Are you Miss Wilcox or Miss Haycastle?'

'Matilda Haycastle,' I said. 'I know it's a daft name, but it's too late to do anything about it now.'

He laughed. 'I'm Jeff Barnes,' he said. 'Marketing Man-

2

ager. One of them, anyway. You're English, aren't you?'

'I'm busy,' I said, tripping the switch. Conversation is difficult when two machines are going full blast. Mr Barnes lingered hopefully for a moment or two, then said, 'See you around,' and wandered off.

Ann giggled. 'He fancies you,' she said. 'Didn't even look at me.' She didn't mind; she was going back to England in a couple of weeks' time with her boyfriend Nigel, and other men were out-of-bounds to her. I wish life were that simple.

Ann and I hadn't known one another before this assignment, but we'd become matey very quickly on a superficial level, the way you can when you're doing a lousy job with someone. She was twenty-five or so, which put her seven or eight years behind me. She and Nigel had been in Brussels for about twelve months, but they hadn't really adapted to the expatriate life. The UK was still 'home' to them and they couldn't wait to get back there. They were going to get married and live in Swindon. I suppose it takes all sorts to make a world.

On our third and last day, Ann was late. She arrived at ten, looking worried. She looked worried all morning. At lunch, her hair was standing on end, she'd run her hands through it so often. She knocked her coffee cup off the table in the canteen, waking everybody up, and then lit a cigarette and promptly dropped that too.

'All right,' I said, picking it up and stubbing it out. I hate cigarette smoke. 'Something's the matter. Tell me about it.'

Whenever I say that, it gets me into trouble.

'It's my friend Connie,' Ann said. 'Well, she's not really a close friend, but we belong to the same theatre group and we did a show together, so I got to know her quite well. She hasn't come back from her holiday.'

My face obviously failed to register sufficient emotion. Across the canteen, Mr Barnes smiled and waved. I smiled back. Ann rushed on, her voice trembling slightly.

'Connie left me her apartment keys and asked me to water her plants and feed her cat and so on while she was

3

in Italy. She was supposed to come back on Sunday. But she hasn't. I left the keys in the letter-box after my last visit. That's what she asked me to do. But when I phoned on Monday to ask if everything was all right, there wasn't any answer, and there was no reply yesterday either. So I went round this morning and managed to get into the building, but when I rang at Connie's front door, there was no reply, except that I could hear Hortense mewing and mewing. That's Connie's cat. But of course I couldn't get in. The lady next door came out and said something, but my French isn't good enough to understand. I don't know what to do.'

I frowned. 'Connie's English?'

Ann nodded.

'Living on her own? No family here?'

She nodded twice more.

'Where does she work?'

'She's a personal assistant in a small office. I can't remember the name, but it's on the Avenue Louise. I've got the phone number.'

'When are they expecting her back? Maybe she's extended her leave, or gone on sabbatical, or something.'

'I never thought of asking them,' Ann said, looking bewildered but slightly reassured. 'Yes, that's possible, I suppose. I'll give them a call after lunch. But what about Hortense? She must be starving.'

'We could go round after work,' I suggested. 'The concierge must have a spare key, or maybe we can get the keys out of the letter-box. We could check out the neighbours as well; maybe they could tell us something.'

'Oh, that's a brilliant idea,' Ann said with some relief. 'I'd forgotten you speak French. I wish I did.'

'I've got no excuse,' I said. 'My mother's French.'

'Lucky thing! I did take French lessons when I first arrived, but I never seemed to get on. Everyone always speaks English, so you never get a chance to practise. And just about every Belgian I meet turns out to be Flemish anyway.'

I should explain here that there are three official lan-

4

guages in Belgium: French, Flemish and German. This is rather a shock to naive foreigners who think their laboriously acquired French will cover all eventualities. You soon discover your mistake when you ask for '*Un café, s'il vous plaît,*' in Flanders. The Flemish are a robust, practical, pushy people, whose contempt for the Walloons dates from 1302, when Flanders knocked the stuffing out of the French at the Battle of the Golden Spurs. They're terrific linguists; nearly all of them speak two if not three of the national languages, plus English. The Walloons on the other hand, like their French cousins, persist in believing that *la langue de Molière* is the only means of communication for civilized people.

The situation is particularly acute in Brussels. To hold a government post, or indeed, almost any job in a Belgian firm, you need to be bilingual. This leads to a preponderance of Flemings in the state sectors and in business, and hence to complaints from the Walloons about unfair competition. Do you begin to get the picture?

When we called Connie's office, a prissy female voice with a slight foreign accent informed us that Miss Trevor was absent on three weeks' vacation. No, the speaker really couldn't say where Miss Trevor was spending her holiday. Ann put the phone down. The worried look was back.

'Connie was only supposed to go to Italy for two weeks,' she said.

'Are you sure?'

She pulled a folded piece of paper out of her bag and handed it to me.

Connie Trevor was obviously a meticulous person. It was a note of instructions, dated two and a half weeks previously. The handwriting was small and careful, on lined exercise-book paper.

Dear Ann,

It's very sweet of you to help me out at such short notice, and Hortense and I appreciate it very much. Between 25 May and 8 June, I'll be contactable at the Villa Rosa in Florence. (There followed an address and telephone number.) I was really lucky to get a room, considering I only made up my mind to go to Italy at the last minute! That'll teach me to make my plans in good time. I'll be back in town on Sunday the 9th, so if you could leave the keys in the mail-box on Saturday, that would be fine. I've stocked the fridge up with food for Hortense. I hope she isn't too naughty. She can go out on the balcony if the weather's good. Don't worry if she climbs on the rail. She only pretends she's going to jump. Could I ask you to bring the mail in every day, otherwise the box gets choked up with all the junk that gets put in? When I get back, I'll take you to my favourite Italian restaurant to say 'Thank you'.

See you in two weeks!'

There followed detailed instructions for watering the plants (from the top, from the bottom, once a week, once a day, remove dead leaves) and for feeding the cat (rabbit flavour on Monday, chicken flavour on Tuesday, salmon Wednesday, don't leave old milk lying around). Salmon flavour? The cat was eating better than I was. At the bottom of the letter Connie had put three crosses and a little sketch of a cat, and had signed for both herself and Hortense.

'How old is Connie?' I asked idly.

'She was forty a couple of months ago. I remember because she was telling me she must be getting near the end of her shelf-life as far as men are concerned.' Ann stopped, frowned, and then added, 'I'm sure she was joking, though. She's quite attractive really.'

At half-past five on the nose, we left the deceitfully glittering foyer for the last time, and headed into town. I have a small fast hatchback, a real city car. Ann closed her eyes and clutched at the seat-belt as we hurtled round Square Montgomery, which is a nightmare at the best of times and the most fiendish of horrors in the rush hour; I have friends who make massive detours all round town in order to avoid it. I have no patience for that sort of thing. I just pretend I'm a Sherman tank. Belgians drive like that all the time and foreigners pick up their habits. You have to, to stay alive. Most male drivers make allowances anyway if you're female and personable. I cash in like mad and get away with murder, which only goes to show how dumb sexism is, especially in men. My only rule is: don't mess with taxi-drivers.

Connie owned an apartment in a rather select, newish building in a quiet street in Woluwe St Pierre. The building had four storeys, with, at a guess, around a dozen apartments of different sizes. The front was a nice dark red brick. Each apartment had a wide balcony with a brass rail and clouded glass panels. Several of the balconies were prettily decorated with window-boxes containing geraniums and petunias. Up top was a penthouse with a large terrace, where cypress trees and assorted greenery waved in the breeze. It looked classy.

It looked even classier inside. The entrance hall was white marble. It had a stone garden with a dead tree in it, and a big mirror flanked by letter-boxes with gold name-plates. Gold metal, anyway. The doorbells were on a small wall-panel. There were twelve apartments, including the concierge's. Connie's was on the second floor at the back.

'What a super place!' Ann said wistfully. 'You just couldn't find anything like this in London.'

'Well, you could,' I said absent-mindedly, studying the mail-boxes. 'But you'd have to be a personal friend of the Queen. Connie's lived in Brussels a while, I take it?'

'Ten years. She bought the flat three years ago.'

Ten years is a long time in a foreign country. Long enough to lose touch with friends and maybe even family. Long enough to lose a sense of identity, if you don't manage to make the transition and build yourself something new. It's OK for people like me, with a foot each side of the Channel. I grew up speaking two languages, have hordes of nosey relatives scattered round northern France, and have been crossing the Strait of Dover like a demented pendulum since I was old enough to be shunted off for the school holidays. Living in different countries just comes naturally. I'd worked in Switzerland and France before coming here, and I'll tell you, after Paris, Brussels is a *morceau de gâteau*: flats, friends and jobs are easy to find, the food's unbelievable and the pace of life is unfrenzied. But I admit that not everyone has had my advantages; and the inhabitants of perfidious Albion have centuries of history to overcome where anything European's concerned. But Connie seemed to have found her feet all right. Ten years on a good salary, only herself and a cat (admittedly a gourmet cat) to keep. The money must have been piling up in the bank. So three years ago she buys herself an apartment.

Buying her own home is an important step for a single woman. It means she's decided to try and make it on her own, instead of waiting for Prince Charming to come along and sweep her off to his boring old castle with gold-plated taps and servants to do the hoovering. It's a recognition that the illusions of youth are finally gone.

The locks on the mail-boxes were derisory. However, I am totally unable to pick a lock and never understand how people in films can whip a bit of bent wire out of their pockets and dissect a Yale in the wink of an eye. But I've lived in Belgium a long time, and I know that the most useful implement for dealing with locked mail-boxes is a wire coat-hanger. With considerable foresight, I'd appropriated one from the visitors' coat cupboard in the office. Before Ann had time to look nervously round, the keys to Connie's flat were in my hand. Ann blinked.

'I never thought of that,' she said.

The lift made pneumatic noises as we went up. It was quiet as we approached the front door of the apartment, but as I put the key in the lock, a cat began to cry pitifully on the other side. She was crouching against the wall of the entrance hall as we came in: a small black cat with golden eyes. She hardly moved when she saw us, and Ann swooped past me with a concerned exclamation and went down on her knees by the animal. I looked round.

8

It was a high-class flat, tastefully decorated in beige and cream, rather too full of knick-knacks and framed photos for my admittedly austere taste. Good furniture, dark brown and expensive. Lots of little tables with bits and pieces in porcelain: china shepherdesses and those appalling sweet-dishes with roses and violets sticking out of the lids. One wall was almost totally glass: a large sliding window which gave on to a balcony with a view of the gardens below.

Ann was rooting around in the kitchen; I heard her talking reassuringly to the cat; the fridge door opened and closed several times. The bedroom was next to the living room and also opened on to the balcony. The décor here was Laura Ashley, with a frilly blue duvet cover and a matching cushion lying on the bed. The bathroom and kitchen were on the inside of the apartment and had no windows, but both were large, well lit and well appointed. There were plenty of fitted cupboards. As I said, a quality place.

Ann was still messing about in the kitchen, so I went in and found her with rubber gloves on. The litter in the tray was soiled through and the cat, in desperation, had resorted to a pile of folded newspapers in one corner. Ann was busy with disinfectant, dustbin bags and fresh cat-litter. A born housewife. Hortense, her nose in the dish, was making up for lost time, presumably with the salmon flavour.

'Look at her. She's desperate,' Ann said. 'I can't believe that Connie would abandon her just like this. It's simply not like her. What are we going to do?'

Outside in the corridor, we heard the lift sigh, and heard the soft clunk of the door opening and closing. There was the sound of muted female voices and then silence. Then the doorbell rang, maniacally loud and shrill; and Ann and I both leapt in the air like champion hurdlers. The cat looked up, then continued to eat, undisturbed. The doorbell rang again.

Ann said again, in a whisper: 'What are we going to do?'

'We'd better open the door,' I said.

I'd left the keys in the lock, on the inside. As I went towards the door, I heard the sound of someone trying unsuccessfully to unlock it from the other side. I yanked it wide open.

There were two middle-aged women in the corridor, with identical looks of concern on their faces. One, clearly the concierge, for she had a bunch of keys in her hand, was short and extremely stout. She had peroxided hair in an untidy beehive, and a squashed-up face with glasses. She wore a flowered cotton overall and had bare legs in flat-soled sandals. She looked like a caricature of Diana Dors.

The other woman, I guessed, was the lady next door. Pleasant round face, pepper-and-salt perm, good quality clothes in various drab shades of beige. She was looking the most apprehensive.

I said: 'Bonjour, Mesdames,' and invited them in.

That reassured them. We were obviously not burglars. The concierge's face cleared even further when she saw Ann. She explained that they had heard the cat mewing and were worried because Madame Trevor had not yet returned from her holidays. I explained that we had also been worried and had come to investigate. We all exclaimed mutually over the plight of the cat, which had now finished eating and was doing an all-over wash. They knew no more than we did. I told them that we thought Connie would probably be away for another week and that we would continue to come in and look after things during that time. I gave the concierge my name and phone number and asked her to call me if Connie should come home. She held the piece of paper at arm's length and studied it carefully, mouthing the syllables of my name. Nobody in continental Europe can pronounce it and she wasn't going to be the exception. Then after mutual well-wishings and reassurances, the two ladies retired.

Ann said: 'Mat, there's just one thing. I'm not going to be here. Since there's no work for the rest of the week, I've changed our flight home. We're leaving tomorrow.'

Guess who was going to be feeding the cat for the next four days?

Chapter 2

My own flat is in Ixelles, near the *Université Libre de Bruxelles*. ULB is the French-speaking university; the Flemish *Vrije Universiteit Brussel* is a short distance away. The university quarter is lively, inexpensive and full of ethnic restaurants and low-priced accommodation. I've lived there ever since I arrived in Brussels seven years ago with my suitcase and five hundred pounds (which were worth a lot more then than they are now). After six wild months in Paris, including a love-affair which still makes me wince to think about it, followed by a cold wet winter wandering bored and lost round a London which I no longer knew, I was only too ready for a change. I sank into the pleasant, undemanding villagey life of Ixelles immediately and have resisted without difficulty the temptation to move to the better-heeled reaches of Woluwe St Pierre or Uccle. I'm on the second floor, and the street down below has Japanese cherry trees which are a perfect glory for about six days every May, if the rain doesn't get them. The park in the Bois de la Cambre is a stone's throw away and you can leave the car in the street quite safely, apart from the dogs that pee on your wheels. What more could you want?

I thought about Connie for a long time that evening, having, for once, nothing better to do with myself. I don't know why the matter was on my mind so much. After all, it was quite possible that Connie had simply decided to stay on in Italy, or to go home to mother, or to go off somewhere else on an impulse. That's what I'd said reassuringly to Ann. So why didn't I believe it myself?

11

The cat, that's why. From what Ann had said, Connie doted on Hortense. The last thing she'd do in the world would be to abandon her. The memory of the desperate mewing came back for a moment, together with the glum thought that, whatever I might tell myself, things were not all well, and that sooner or later, someone, probably me, was going to have to do something about it. Like going to the police.

I don't like the police. This isn't because I've been in trouble myself, as so-called friends have laughingly suggested, because I haven't. My record is, as they say here, virgin. But I nearly married a copper who turned out to be crooked, and the experience has left me prejudiced against both marriage and the police-force, in about equal measure. And in Belgium, nobody goes to the police about anything unless they absolutely have to.

Furthermore, I wouldn't even know whom to go to. The situation here is somewhat complicated. The communal or local police have a reputation for being thuggish and trigger-happy; indeed, at one time they notched up such a healthy score of innocent bystanders that questions were asked. I gather things have improved since then, but I didn't want to be the one to put it to the test. The national *Gendarmerie*, which is part of the armed forces, is generally reckoned to be more reliable and better trained. Then you have the *Police Judiciaire*, who carry out criminal investigation on behalf of the courts. All these bodies tend to overlap and they tread on one another's toes to a highly confusing extent. It was a tangle I didn't want to get involved in.

At this point, I got a piece of paper and a ball-point pen and sat down to think properly. This wasn't my responsibility. I didn't even know Connie. There was her family, first of all. There were her employers. And thirdly, there were her friends. She must have friends after being in town for ten years. All of those were avenues to follow up. I had four free days to do it in.

I then wrote down all the information Ann had given me about Connie. Forty. Single. No boyfriend, as far as

12

Ann knew. Father and mother dead. Yes, that's right, the mother had died three or four years ago, but there was a married sister living in the Home Counties somewhere. A member of several of the expatriate amateur dramatic/choral societies with which Brussels bristles. Had worked for an English company originally, then for the European Commission, then for the last three years as personal assistant in a small firm in the Avenue Louise. I had the number. There was enough there to be going on with. Connie's flat might also provide more information.

Feeling happier at having done something positive, I took myself downtown and went to see *Once Upon a Time in the West* for the fifth time. It was the long version where Cheyenne dies and I was the only person in the cinema, apart from the projectionist, the usherette and the lady selling the tickets. The whole magnificent saga unfolded in its unhurried way for me alone. They locked the door behind me when I left, with a cheery *'Bonne nuit, Madame!'* and I worried about their profit margins all the way home.

A totally different cat greeted me early the next morning when I opened the door to Connie's apartment. Perhaps 'greet' is the wrong word. Hortense was obviously a cat of considerable character. She sniffed round my shoes, gave me a haughty glance, then walked languidly to the fridge door and sat there, waiting. After receiving her food, she took no further notice of me at all, but retired to a sunny patch on the carpet and went to sleep. Fine. Nobody to bother me.

I have to say that I did feel a qualm or two about rifling through Connie's personal possessions. On the other hand, someone had to do something. I stifled the qualms.

There was nothing at all of interest in the bedroom or kitchen. All Connie's papers were in a small wooden cabinet in the living room, filed away in transparent plastic folders, each one with a label. The papers pertaining to the purchase of the apartment, mortgage agreement, utilities and phone, television licence and cable fee, just as you would expect. Insurance policies, together with a complete inventory, neatly typed, of all the furniture and ornaments in the flat, with values in the right-hand column. Income tax declarations for the past five years, as required by law. Connie was earning a nice solid salary, but nothing outrageous by Brussels standards. Employment contract, payslips, details of social security payments and contributions to medical insurance, pension statements, bank statements, neatly filed in the little green folders which the bank gives you and which I always lose. In fact, all the paperwork associated with an average working life and nothing unusual. The only unusual thing was that there was nothing personal in the cabinet at all.

In my experience, people, particularly female people, acquire over the years a whole lot of paper to which they are particularly attached and with which they wouldn't part under any circumstances. Family correspondence, love-letters, Christmas and birthday cards, holiday souvenirs, theatre programmes and menus of special meals: things which soon lose their significance and hang about, like autumn leaves which look so brilliant at first but soon go brown, or dull sea-shells once bright from the water. They're the fingerprints of moments of special emotional significance, and Connie hadn't kept a single one. I couldn't believe it. You have to have the emotional make-up of Attila the Hun not to have a few mementoes of things past in your cupboard; even I have one or two.

At this stage, I began to want to know more about Connie. I got up and collected all the photos that decorated the apartment in such profusion. Most of them were of groups of smiling people taken during theatrical productions of one sort or another, but there were one or two snow scenes, with everyone balanced precariously on unaccustomed skis, muffled up in snow-goggles and those silly knitted hats with pom-poms on the top. The four which interested me most were family ones. These were in silver frames. There was one of three women, smiling, their arms around each other in front of a mantelpiece decorated with Christmas cards. The family resemblance was marked: mother and two daughters, all with the same type of slightly frizzy fair hair. A wedding photo with smiling bride and groom completed the identification: Connie was the plain one, as luck would have it. Plain but pleasant-looking, with an open face, blue eyes and a cheery smile. The married sister was just that bit prettier, just that bit taller and slimmer. The last two pictures were of babies. You'd have had to be related to find them appealing. One was inscribed: 'To Auntie Connie from Bobby' and the other: 'To Auntie Connie from Lucy'. Original.

I replaced the photos and went to the window to look out. Although still early, it was already hot. Hortense got up, stretched, and idly followed me. At the window, she looked up and gave a small, interrogative mew. Then she looked at the window again. Aha. I was learning the language. I pulled the stiff window open about six inches, and she slipped through like a silk scarf and jumped up on the balcony rail with the nonchalance of Nijinsky. A blackbird rose from the garden below, shrilling in alarm, and Hortense looked at it with slitted eyes and made a chattering noise between her teeth. Cats have uncivilized impulses.

What had I learned? Not a lot. I now knew the name of the company Connie worked for: Sundsvall International. It was a small Swedish outpost office which monitored events in the EC and lobbied on behalf of Head Office in Stockholm. They were something to do with the paper industry. Connie's job was described as 'Personal Assistant to the International Marketing Manager', which sounded grand, but probably wasn't. What else was there?

A bookcase full of standard classics, with a majority of female authors. Lots of Brontës, Jane Austens and George Eliots, and every single blessed book ever written by Georgette Heyer. I was just about to turn away when I saw the photograph albums.

There were six of them: the record of a life. Connie was incredible. Every photo was dated on the back in that same meticulous handwriting, and many of them had a cheery little caption written underneath. The record started on 5 April 1983, the date of Connie's arrival in Belgium (first voyage on a hovercraft). At first, the pages were filled with Brussels scenes: the Grand'Place, the Manneken Pis, the Atomium, the parks, the antiques market in the Sablon and so on. Many of them were very good; Connie obviously had an eye. None of this first sequence, which lasted right through the summer and autumn, were of people, except for half a dozen in August, when the sister came to visit. Connie on Ostend beach. Linda on the steps of the cathedral. Linda.

Connie had gone home for Christmas that first year. I recognized the small-format version of the framed picture with mother and sister. There were quite a lot more, of jolly smiles under paper hats, a large, bronzed turkey on the table, paper-chains getting in people's way. Then a Polaroid picture of a New Year's Eve party, with both sisters and everyone else rollickingly drunk, caught red-eyed in the flash like animals in the headlights of a car.

In the spring of '84, Connie had got involved with the Brussels amateur theatrical scene. A succession of productions was recorded: she had started off doing back-stage work, then progressed to small non-speaking parts in pantomimes and Shakespeare. Life seemed to have been a lot of fun. That summer she went to Greece, on what looked like an archaeological tour of classical sites; there were pictures of people in shorts and sandals grinning enthusiastically in front of Corinthian columns. More theatrical activities in the autumn, pictures taken late at night at cast parties or in cheap restaurants, with everyone jammed together eating spaghetti bolognese and drinking Chianti and enjoying themselves hugely. Then Christmas in England again.

And now another name. Another New Year's Eve party, obviously, but at the side was written 'Mick home from Australia at last' with an arrow pointing to a vaguely male shape at the back of the room. On the next page were four photos of a young man with a deep tan and rather thick, untidy fair hair. This was a long way from the Home Counties; the colours of the land were bright and alien: Australia, I supposed. Mick riding, Mick surfing, Mick at the wheel of a Land-Rover, Mick smiling at the camera. He was very attractive.

The next sequence was predictable, I suppose. Mick and Connie on romantic weekends in England at first, then Mick and Connie in Brussels. Photos in Bruges, in Ghent, in the lovely green-valleyed country around the Meuse, which tourists never dream is there. Grey stone towns on the tranquil river bank; castles on hilltops guarding the valleys; churches with peculiar onion-shaped domes huddled against cliff-faces. It lasted all through the spring and summer, Connie's romance. The best picture was taken at a fancy-dress ball: Mick in Aristide Bruant cloak and hat, and Connie in an amazing electric-blue fringed twenties dress, radiant, delphinium-eyed, confident.

It was over by the autumn of '85. The last picture of them together was on holiday, on a café terrace with mountains in the background; Ticino, or Italy maybe. She may have asked a waiter or someone at the next table to take it. She was smiling at the camera, but he was looking off to one side, morose behind sun-glasses.

There was a long time gap then. The next photograph, which followed immediately in the album, was dated autumn 1986, and belonged to the wedding sequence. These were recognizably the work of a professional photographer. Linda and Dave outside the church, together in the garden, with Connie and her mother, with bridesmaids, with wedding guests. Inevitably, Connie was a bridesmaid. The get-up didn't suit her. Maybe bridesmaids' outfits are specially designed so as to flatter the bride. Connie looked older, rather faded, her mouth a little set.

Then there was a second time gap. The photos resumed in early '88, and from then on they were fewer, and nearly all theatrical or scenic holiday snaps. There were a few pictures of the babies, but no other family pictures and no more trips home for Christmas. The most recent ones were some beautiful studies of Hortense. The last picture of Connie herself had been taken after a pantomime at the beginning of the year; she looked rather tired and it had obviously been an effort to smile. She looked every minute of forty years old.

I sat back, somewhat reflectively. Two major gaps in the record: the year before the wedding and the year and a half after. Why hadn't Connie recorded those periods of her life?

It was quiet in the apartment; very little noise came in through the slightly opened window. I shivered a little; and at the same moment, the cat gave a forlorn howl which made my scalp twitch. The sound rose and fell, not loud, but disturbing in its alienness. I'd never heard a cat call like that before. As she howled again, I propelled myself out of the chair and got on my knees beside her. She was crouching just inside the window, head low on the carpet. I spoke her name and stroked her. She didn't respond much, but at least the howling stopped. My heart was beating quickly. A moment later she looked round at me, took a quick lick at the place where my hand had been, and sat up in a more normal position.

I started to feel jumpy. I wanted to get out of the apartment. But I still needed information. Names, addresses, telephone numbers. Surely someone as organized as Connie would have an address book in the flat? By the telephone probably. Right again, Matilda. I wanted the sister's number in England. I didn't know the surname, so I went right through the book, and found it under 'H'. Connie had written 'Linda and David' and underneath was an address and phone number. You don't write the surnames of your own relatives. I copied the information down quickly, put everything away where I'd found it, and got out of there, feeling relieved and guilty at the same time. I felt bad about the cat, though.

Chapter 3

Back home, I tried the Florence number first. Getting through to Italy was the usual pain in the backside; when I succeeded, after fifteen minutes, I couldn't get hold of anyone who spoke anything but Italian. I don't speak Italian, apart from '*Pronto*'. No go. I absolutely don't understand why telephoning Italy is such hard labour. Anyone would think it's on the moon. But it was obviously important to establish first of all that Connie hadn't simply decided to stay on in Florence. I needed an interpreter.

In a city like Brussels, that's no problem. I made a quick phone call and in five minutes was on my way to the luxurious home of my beautiful friend Giulia. Giulia, who would make the water on Botticelli's knees boil, is the wife of a rich young Italian diplomat. They live in a house with a Horta staircase, and I pitched up on their doorstep one day to photograph it for a friend of mine, who was writing a book on Brussels art nouveau. Both Giulia and Antonio are art nouveau freaks and so am I. In fact, I've been having a major romance with Victor Horta ever since I visited his Brussels house, now a museum, and fell wildly in love with all that sublime *fin-de-siècle* elegance. Art nouveau really took off in turn-of-the-century Brussels, and luckily even the rabid zeal of the modern redevelopers hasn't quite managed to wipe out all of it. My friend's book never got written because her husband's company moved them to Philadelphia, but I now have a wonderful collection of pictures of Giulia's staircase, which like everything else in her house is ravishing. Giulia herself thought I was from *Vogue* magazine at first, but we quickly became friends after we'd got that one sorted out. I get invited to dinner whenever they want to prove to Italian male chauvinist friends that Englishwomen don't all look like horses.

I found Giulia, as usual, looking as if she'd just stepped out of Valentino's showroom, and explained what I needed. There was no nonsense. She picked up one of the telephones and blasted her way through the Italian system in fifty seconds flat. There ensued a long conversation at maximum volume, with hand gestures. Then she slammed the phone down and sat for a moment in silence.

'Well?' I said.

'She is not there. She was there, but she is not there now. She left on Saturday afternoon to catch the overnight train to Brussels. She had a first-class ticket for a sleeping car. They were sorry to see her go, because she was such a nice, quiet lady. You know, Matilda, that tells me exactly what kind of place it is. Two elderly ladies with a house that is too big and not enough plumbing.' Giulia shivered extravagantly and gave me a big smile. 'Are you happy now, Matilda darling? Shall we have a sherry? I have a new piece of Lalique to show you.'

I always leave Giulia's house feeling as if I sleep on the streets. It takes a minute or two to reflate my ego.

Back home, I took a deep breath and picked up the phone to call Connie's sister in England. I'd sat looking at the phone for a long time before doing this, wondering why I was interfering. Then I dialled the number, in Guildford. A pleasant female voice answered almost immediately: 'Linda Harrison.' I like people who introduce themselves on the phone.

I'd thought for a while about how to present the problem and had decided to opt for pretended ignorance. Accordingly, I said in a bright girlish voice: 'Oh, good morning. May I speak to Connie Trevor, please?'

There was a moment's startled pause at the other end, then the voice said: 'But Connie's not here. This is her sister Linda.'

'But I thought she was on holiday in England,' I said. 'I'm a friend of Connie's in Brussels – well, actually I'm a friend of a friend – and I was sure she said . . . Oh dear, it must have been a mistake. I am sorry to have bothered you. You don't happen to know where Connie is, do you? I mean, it's nothing very urgent, but I would like to . . .' I trailed off and waited.

'Well, as far as I know, she's in Brussels, unless she's still on holiday. We had a postcard from Italy a week or so ago and I don't know exactly when she's getting back. I'll give you her Brussels number and you can try there.' She then gave me the number of Connie's flat.

'That's very kind of you,' I said. 'If by any chance Connie should phone you, would you mind asking her to give me a call?' I then gave her my name and number, we thanked one another and rang off. She sounded like a nice lady.

Double zero.

It was time for a very late lunch. My stomach had been grumbling for a while; Giulia's excellent sherry was feeling lonely. I ate, ruminating. The phone rang; it was the temp agency with an assignment for the following week. A company on the Avenue des Arts needed some-one to type labels. I suppose all the regular secretaries had refused, or said they were too busy, which comes to the same thing. I accepted. I eke out the temp work with a bit of editing and proof-reading, but there wasn't a lot going on just then. Enough to pay the rent. Sometimes I think I should consider taking a permanent job, but I've never been much good at saluting other people's flags. I don't worry too much about it.

Connie's office was my next target. When the prissy voice answered, I said: 'Oh, hello. May I speak to Mr Smith, please?'

This is standard secretarial technique when you can't read your boss's handwriting or can't remember whether he said Smith, Jones or Gruntington-Hythe and don't want to make a fool of yourself by asking. A helpful telephone operator will give you the names of all the executives in the office if you go about it the right way.

I had to repeat it.

· 'We have no Mr Smith working here,' the voice said. I placed the accent: Swedish, logically enough.

'Oh, but this is the number I was given,' I said, affronted, and laboriously spelled it out. The prissy lady said, faint exasperation creeping in: 'I tell you, we have no Mr Smith working here. We have a Mr Jarnstedt and a Mr Robinson. That is all. You have made a mistake.'

She put the phone down in the middle of my apology. However, she'd saved me the trouble of asking what the gentlemen in the office were called, which is the next step. I'm thinking of patenting this technique; it never fails. Incidentally, if by chance there is a Mr Smith in the office (which does happen), you ask which Mr Smith and say you need another Mr Smith.

At two-thirty I was at the door of the office, armed with an executive briefcase. It wasn't a real office-block, but an apartment building, two floors of which had been converted for office use. There was the usual dead tree in the foyer, and the inner door was firmly locked. I was searching for the right doorbell and had just located it when a young man in shirt-sleeves breezed in with a clipboard under his arm. A small courier's van was parked at the kerb outside, engine throbbing, just like in the movies. The young man grinned at me, stabbed at the doorbell with his finger, announced the name of his firm, and headed for the inner door as the buzzer went. I headed briskly in with him. We took the lift together.

The courier and I got out at the same floor. We made for the same door, which bore an extremely businesslike lock. He rang, and the door opened almost immediately. I had no trouble identifying the prissy lady. Her dress suggested the little girl, with a full skirt, a short jacket and a white-collared blouse. She wore her hair shoulder-length, in a wide velvet Alice band, and her make-up was very discreet. She was no spring chicken though. The skin round her eyes was thin and papery, and I put her age in the early forties, despite the girlish dress.

The outer door led into a small foyer and there was yet another security door to get through before gaining access to the office. The international business community has been paranoid about terrorism since the Gulf War. I wouldn't have thought the Swedish paper industry was a major target, but these days you never know. I mightn't have got in at all if it hadn't been for the courier, who was obviously a regular visitor. He went straight through to pick up his package, and I followed straight in after, before the prissy lady could say anything. She came trotting after us hastily, looking put out.

'May I help you?' she asked. The frost in her voice would have chilled a polar bear.

'I'm looking for Connie Trevor,' I said. 'I understand she works here.'

Was I mistaken, or did the papery features tighten slightly?

'Miss Trevor is on vacation,' she said. 'You will have to come back next week.'

'It's really very urgent,' I said. 'Could you tell me where I can get hold of her?'

The courier left with a smile and a nod, ignored by both of us.

'No, I cannot,' the woman said, definitely unfriendly now. 'She did not inform me where she was going.'

'Are you Mr Jarnstedt's secretary?' I asked.

'I am the Office Manager,' she said with icy dignity. 'Miss Trevor is Mr Robinson's secretary.'

'Oh? I thought she was his personal assistant?'

'She likes to call herself a personal assistant, but she is nothing but an overpaid secretary really.'

I was a little surprised at the vindictiveness in her voice. I'd obviously stumbled on a sore point. I decided to push a little further.

'Is Mr Robinson in?' I asked. 'I'd like a word with him.'

She said nothing for a long moment, staring at me with cold eyes. Then she said: 'He will not be back till very late.'

I had the feeling she was lying. Maybe the pause had been just a fraction too long. Maybe it was the flicker of a glance she directed at the clock on the wall. It was a quarter to three; if Robinson had been out for lunch, he'd surely be back soon. Ignoring the two open doors, I sat down in a leather armchair in the small reception area and smiled up at my opponent.

'I think I'll just wait for him,' I said. 'I've got nothing else to do today.'

She flushed angrily and then became quite white. 'He will not be in the office at all this afternoon,' she told me. 'There is really no point for you to wait.'

'That's all right,' I replied.

Her voice became louder. 'He will not see you!'

'I thought you said he wasn't coming back?' I said mildly.

For a moment she stared at me furiously, then with a flounce of her full skirts, she turned abruptly, went out and slammed the entrance door, came in and slammed the inner door, and then disappeared into her own office, behind opaque glass walls. The sound of an angry typewriter began.

I waited for about twenty minutes, hoping that I wouldn't have to spend the whole afternoon in that dreary place. The office was small and not too well lit. Despite the double-glazing, the sound of the traffic on the busy Avenue Louise filtered through: the hooting of irritable taxis, the throb of diesel delivery vans and the incessant revving of stopping and starting cars. The Office Manager emerged once, threw another furious glance at me, and disappeared again to resume her frenetic typing.

Then abruptly, there came the sound of voices outside and the door opened to admit two men, both in business suits. One was tall and dark with a moustache; the other pear-shaped and slightly balding. I stood up. The Office Manager surged out of her office and said angrily: 'Mr Robinson, this woman will not go away. I have told her you will not see her but she insists on staying.'

Both men looked startled and confused, as well they might. I said, in a calm voice: 'Mr Robinson?' and the podgy man said cautiously: 'Yes?'

'My name's Matilda Haycastle,' I said. 'I'd appreciate ten minutes of your time. It's about your assistant, Connie Trevor.'

'Connie?' he said. 'Oh, well, won't you come in, Miss er . . .?'

Nobody ever gets it first time.

A minute or two later, I was sitting in front of his desk. He asked the Office Manager to bring coffee, which she did with extremely bad grace, slapping the cup down in front of me so that the liquid spilled into the saucer. She had put little blue folded napkins into the saucers under each cup. Another obsessively neat personality, just like Connie.

I said: 'I'm afraid your Office Manager thinks I'm up to no good.'

'Oh, that's just Karin,' he replied. 'She can be rather difficult sometimes.'

'She doesn't seem to like Connie too much either,' I remarked, hoping it sounded artless.

'They've had a few disagreements,' he said, the cautious tone still in his voice. 'Women don't seem to be able to get on together, especially when they're a certain age.'

He suddenly remembered he was talking to a woman, and one of a certain age at that, and he looked confused. He had an unformed face and a round head like a baby's. He wasn't my idea of an international executive. He was sweating slightly, and his shirt buttons were under a definite strain. The office lunches can be fierce in Brussels.

'How can I help you?' he asked.

I decided to tell the truth.

'I'm worried because Connie hasn't come home after her holiday in Italy, and I was hoping you could give me some idea of where she might be and who her friends are.'

'Hasn't come home?' he asked, startled.

I gave a brief résumé of the situation. He looked genuinely concerned. An honest man, I thought, if not a stylish one.

'I'm afraid I really don't have much of an idea about

Connie's private life,' he said, leaning back in his chair. 'She was my predecessor's secretary and I inherited her when I came here a year ago. She's an extremely efficient secretary.'

There was a 'but' in his voice.

'But?' I asked.

'Rather moody,' he said. 'Sometimes you just can't talk to her. Then it all clears up and she's fine again. As to what she does in her spare time, I know she's involved with one of the amateur dramatic societies, but I don't remember her ever talking about her friends.'

'And you've never asked?'

He looked uncomfortable. 'I don't like prying,' he said. He added, rather ruefully: 'I'm not exactly a brilliant communicator myself.'

'Would Karin know anything?' I asked. A long shot, but worth trying.

'God, no!' Robinson said feelingly. 'They're not even on speaking terms any more. I sometimes think they hate each other.'

'It's rather a small office for people not to be on speaking terms,' I said gently.

'The trouble is that we don't really need two support staff,' he said, rather despairingly. 'We need one really good multilingual person. Karin's written English is poor and so are her secretarial skills, but she set the office up and she's been here for eight years. Connie's a most efficient secretary but she doesn't speak Swedish. We've been hoping that one of them will leave, but so far, they're both hanging on.'

'They're probably both terrified of losing their jobs and madly jealous of one another,' I said.

'I suppose so,' he said glumly. 'I'd keep Connie on if I had the choice, but Karin's divorced with a child to bring up. One can't just get rid of her.'

No, I thought, it's easier to avoid making a management decision and let them go on snapping and snarling like two animals in the same cage. I thought about all the days in three years, all the days of animosity, obstructiveness, spite; the million petty ways of making someone's life a misery; the constant irritations rubbing deeper and deeper. I thought of the crumpled, resentful face of the woman in the outer office and I shivered just a little.

'Listen,' I said, 'I may be worrying about nothing, and Connie may still turn up safe and sound. But if she doesn't come to work next Monday, will you notify the police?'

'The police?' he repeated, startled. 'Do you really think . . .'

'She may have had an accident,' I said. 'They're better equipped to find out about that sort of thing.'

'Well, I suppose, if she doesn't come in on Monday, we'll have to think about it,' he said reluctantly. 'Or maybe I could call the British Embassy?'

'Whatever,' I said. 'As long as you do something.'

The typewriter was still chattering away angrily as I came out. I let myself out and was surprised to find the sun shining in the street. I felt as if I'd been buried alive, like those two women.

The taste was still in my mouth that evening, so I took myself downtown for a drink, fell in with some friends, and ended up around eight o'clock in one of the Irish pubs around the Rond-Point Schuman, where a number of the European Commission offices are. It was a quiet Thursday night with only a few punters in. The Commission area is an ant-hill during the day, what with the roadworks and the construction of the new Parliament buildings and the toing and froing between the different offices, but at night, it's the elephants' graveyard.

Two glasses of indifferent white wine are about as much as I can stand. At half-past eight I went to the bar to get a Perrier and a man who was sitting there reading the *Daily Telegraph* looked up and said: 'Well, hello.'

It was Jeff Barnes. He put his paper down with a certain eagerness and smiled. He was, as I have said, an attractive man. I like tall men. I'm tall myself and I like to be able to look a man in the eye.

'Miss Haycastle,' he said. 'That's the name, isn't it? The intrepid temp?'

I smiled back. 'It's Matilda. What's intrepid about me?'

'Everything,' he said. 'You put the wind up the office dragon all right. We're all still reeling. May I buy you a drink?'

Fifteen minutes later, my friends took their leave, and Jeff and I proceeded to a cheerful student restaurant near the Ixelles cemetery, where the food is plentiful and cheap and you can do the crossword on the paper place-mat while you're waiting for your order to arrive. It was my suggestion. Jeff had only been in town for a couple of months and didn't know any places yet. He was filled with the exuberance of a man enjoying himself for the first time in a while; and I found him good company. The place was packed and very lively and we had a lot to drink. I have a good head for alcohol; it runs in the family. I was sober enough to turn down the proposition politely, when it came. Jeff, less cool, said unguardedly: 'Why? Is it because I'm married?'

He hadn't meant to tell me that and he winced. So did I.

'Are you?' I asked. Just my luck, though I should have known. Nine out of ten of them are married. However, some of them are gentleman enough to tell you at the beginning of the evening.

He looked down at the table.

'My wife's staying in England.' He sounded a lot more sober now. 'She's got a good job and the kids are happy at school and she doesn't feel like moving. I go home every other weekend.'

That kind of arrangement is commoner out here than you'd think. Not every executive wife is ready to uproot herself at the snap of a corporation's fingers. Unfortunately, the result is often a total disruption of family life. The wife and kids have to learn to manage on their own and frequently succeed only too well, while the husband shuttles back and forth across the Channel, unable to make a real life for himself in Brussels yet finding that he's an unwelcome stranger when he gets home.

'You'll get fed up with that in six months,' I told Jeff Barnes. 'England's not far away on paper, but that

Channel gets to be like the Himalayas after a while. And once you start making friends and getting into the swing here, you won't feel like going back at all. Tell your wife to get her body over here. It's a great life.'

He grinned ruefully.

'You're so different,' he said. 'You're exciting. I can't imagine my wife talking like that.'

I always know when it's time to go home. I dropped him, rather silent, outside his service flat, and broke the speed-limit all the way home. We'd made no arrangements to meet again. I like my men unattached, and when no one suitable is about, I'm prepared to wait. Sleeping alone doesn't bother me.

Chapter 4

I slept late on Friday. I'd gone as far as I could with Connie for the time being, so I put her aside to simmer, as it were, and used the day profitably. It's fun being free when everyone else is working. I took Giulia out for lunch to thank her for her efforts the previous day. We went slumming (for her, anyway) in a Vietnamese café full of fat, cheerful children, who amused her greatly. Giulia laughs a lot; I think that's why she's so beautiful. The waiters thought she was marvellous.

I kept my trips to Connie's flat short, because I was beginning to dread them. Hortense wasn't eating much, and scarcely seemed to take any notice when I came in, nor did she respond to my attempts to talk to her. I hoped she was all right. I didn't want Connie coming home to find that her cat had pined away like a consumptive Victorian virgin. I made one other discovery, which might have meant something or not. I remembered to check the bathroom, thinking that there might be some clue to Connie's state of health, if not her mind. The cabinet was full of natural remedies for everything from headaches to constipation, but at the back I found an unopened pack containing three months' supply of contraceptive pills. I looked at them for a while. A woman of forty doesn't stay on the pill without good reason; the reason is usually the obvious one: that she's sexually active. I frowned. It didn't chime with what I'd heard about Connie. But, on the other hand, there might be medical reasons I knew nothing about. File it away for future reference.

I kept telling myself that Connie was coming home

because I didn't really see the way ahead if she didn't. I could hardly walk into a police station and report the disappearance of someone I'd never even met. So I put the whole business out of my mind as best I could and enjoyed my weekend. The sun shone, which isn't all that usual in Belgium in the summer. I went to a barbecue in someone's field of a garden and we sat talking round the campfire nearly all night and drove home as the sun rose again, the streets empty except for the first Sunday tram and the blackbirds singing like sopranos.

Monday was a bad day. I turned up for the job and found that the addresses I had to type were all in Tokyo, that the typewriter was a manual one left over from the Dark Ages, and that my office companion was an elderly spinster who brought her poodle to work with her. I bashed away all day with the blasted dog staring beadily at me over the rim of the desk and got out on the dot of five-thirty to go to Connie's, hoping against hope to find that she'd got home safely. But to my dismay, no one answered the doorbell. I opened the mail-box, shoved the contents into the side pocket of my handbag, went up in the lift and entered the apartment to find that the whole place had been turned upside down.

I can't really describe the different sensations that I experienced. I think the first was disbelief, that I'd walked into the wrong apartment by mistake, that I was seeing things, that it hadn't really happened. The next thing I felt was a wave of sheer panic, which sent me rocketing out and down the stairs, ignoring the lift, terrified that whoever had done it might come after me. My handbag caught on the end of the stair-rail and I wrenched it free, breaking the strap. Then I found myself outside the concierge's flat in the basement, ringing the doorbell and pounding like an idiot, and when she came to the door, I could hardly get the words out, I was shaking so much.

Madame and Monsieur were very matter-of-fact about it. They sat me down and gave me a very small shot of brandy, listened to a more coherent version, and then, as I was slowly getting back into my skin, Madame said that her husband would go up and see what had happened and she would then ring the police. Monsieur, who was about six foot six and correspondingly broad, plucked a large hockey-stick out of a cupboard, turned to me with a cheerful wink and said that if there was anyone up there, they'd soon wish they weren't. Feeling much braver, I said I'd go with him, and we went solemnly up in the lift, by which time I was feeling rather foolish at having lost my cool. The truth was that this whole damn business was getting on my nerves.

There was no one in the apartment, of course. I stood nervously by the door while Monsieur picked his way through the rubble to investigate the various rooms. Then we went back downstairs, locking the door behind us, and sat waiting for the police to arrive. My brain was functioning again; I took the opportunity to ask if Madame Trevor had a '*petit ami*', a regular gentleman friend. No, not for the three years they'd known her. There had been ordinary friends of course, but no one special. Did she stay out at all at night? No, though sometimes she came home very late. She was a quiet, pleasant lady, Madame Trevor, never caused any trouble at all. The bell rang; the moment I'd been dreading arrived.

I was slightly reassured to see that the two large agents who loomed into the small entrance hall were from the *Gendarmerie* rather than the communal police. These two were extremely businesslike. They listened to us, apparently unconcerned, taking notes. So Madame Trevor was away? Where? When was she due back? I let the concierge answer the questions as much as possible; it had suddenly occurred to me that the police might realize that I knew rather too much about Connie's disappearance. I therefore kept quiet when they said that they would make enquiries and no doubt Madame Trevor would soon be found and notified, and that we would be expected to make official statements and to contribute our fingerprints in due course. Then they put their notebooks away and we all went up to the apartment to take a look.

Casting another, more intensive glance around, I saw

that the mess was total. All Connie's papers had been taken out and scattered about; drawers and cabinets had all been emptied. Some of the ornaments had even been thrown down and smashed. It was impossible to say whether anything had been taken. The police told us not to touch anything; the fingerprint people would have to check the place. I suddenly remembered with a flip-flop of my stomach that I had probably left mine everywhere. I had a ludicrous impulse to whip out my hanky and start dusting. Too late.

We were just about to retire again when I suddenly remembered Hortense. At the same moment, Madame Boxus, the concierge (we had introduced ourselves by now) said: '*Mais où est le chat?*'

Hortense was nowhere to be found, though Madame Boxus and I went into every room and searched as best we could, calling her name and trying not to touch anything. Finally I had the thought of looking outside on the balcony. I slid the window open and went out. Nothing. I could hear Madame Boxus still calling hopefully: '*Minou, minou!*' inside the flat.

One of the cops poked his head out.

'Anything?'

'No.'

'In the garden?' he asked, emerging.

'She doesn't go out,' I replied automatically.

'*C'est quoi, alors?*' he said, pointing downwards.

I looked. A small black object was crouching quite still in the gay flowerbed under the balconies. Oh God! Hortense!

For the second time that day, I flew all the way down the stairs without bothering the lift, found my way out to the back garden, and knelt beside the cat. She hadn't moved. She was alive, but strangely rigid, shivering. I felt her over carefully. There didn't seem to be any bones broken, but then I wasn't a vet.

'Is it dead?' Madame Boxus cried shrilly from above. I looked up and saw the four heads peering over the edge of the balcony. Heads were beginning to appear on other balconies, too. The visit of policemen was too exciting to be missed. There might be an arrest, with any luck. *Quel scandale!*

'No,' I called back. 'I think she's just shocked.'

I picked Hortense up carefully and carried her back inside. Upstairs, the policemen were preparing to leave. They looked at the cat in my arms and scratched their heads.

'Well, now we've found it, what are we going to do with it?' one of them said. 'We can't leave it here.'

Everybody looked at me.

I drove home with an earth-bowl, several tons of kitty-litter, a month's supply of cat food, and Hortense silent in a wicker cat-basket. The police had taken the apartment keys.

Hortense didn't like my flat.

The police came round the next day for a statement about the break-in, which I gave them, leaving out all about my researches into Connie's whereabouts. They also took my fingerprints, and relieved me of Connie's letter to Ann Wilcox. I'd had the foresight to make a photocopy for my own files, but I didn't tell them that. I asked if their enquiries had got anywhere, and received shrugs and non-committal faces in reply. No doubt, they said, I would hear more in the fullness of time.

Chapter 5

As it happened, I heard in the shortness of time. It was
Wednesday, early evening. The mind-blowing boredom of
my day's work had left me with a surplus of energy. I
did some shopping, took my handbag round to the local
cobbler's to have the broken strap mended, and was busy
cleaning my windows when the doorbell rang. The apartment doorbell, not the bell downstairs. I stopped dead
where I sat, perched on the window-sill with one leg out.
The concierge? Jehovah's Witnesses? Swinging my leg
inside, I crossed to the door and peered out through the
fish-eye.

The man outside wasn't in uniform; but even the dis-
torted image in the spy-hole had policeman written all
over it. Nobody else gets inside buildings so easily. I was
damned if I was going to open the door without a struggle,
so I called: 'Yes?' and waited.

He turned towards the door, his head looming large
and grotesque in the glass eye. He answered in English,
muffled, but I caught the word 'police', though I didn't
catch his name, which was long and Flemish.

'Identity card,' I yelled.

There was a moment's silence outside. They're not used
to being asked for ID. I wondered if he'd comply, or
simply kick the door down. However, I needn't have
worried. He moved and bent down, and a plastic-covered
card slid under the door.

He was from the *Police Judiciaire*. Luc Vanderauwera,
Inspecteur Principal.

I took a deep breath. Then I opened the door.

If I hadn't known he was a policeman, I might have thought he was one of the opposition. He looked tough. He was a couple of inches taller than I, about the same age, brown-haired, blue-eyed. He looked bored and bad-tempered.

'I came earlier, but you weren't in,' he said, abruptly. His English was excellent; he had mastered the apostrophe, and I also thought I could detect a slight south London accent. I recognize it because I've got a touch of the transpontine whine myself now and then.

'I work,' I said, equally abruptly.

Whisking the ID card out of my hand, he walked into the flat as if he owned it, then stopped and turned to look at me. I don't suppose I was a particularly appealing sight in my house-cleaning clothes, my hair knotted up in one of those turbans that Clementine Churchill and charladies used to wear. I closed the door and returned the stare.

'I was looking at your statement,' he said without preamble. 'I've got a few questions.'

'Ask,' I said, folding my arms.

I hadn't invited him to sit down. He moved over to my bookcases and studied them. I stayed where I was.

'Why did you phone Miss Trevor's sister?' he asked casually.

They'd got there on their own. Maybe they weren't as dumb as popular legend would have it, after all. Tell the truth, Matilda.

'To find out if Connie was there,' I said.

'You're a friend of Miss Trevor's?'

'No. I've never met her.'

'So why did you call?'

'I knew she hadn't come home. It seemed rather strange, so I thought I'd make a few enquiries.'

'You went to her office and caused a scene.'

Caught by surprise, I couldn't help giving a gasp, half of astonished laughter.

'A scene? Who told you that?'

'Was it you who called Italy too?'

'No, it was an Italian friend of mine.'

36

'If you didn't know Miss Trevor, why did you go to all that trouble?'

The questions and answers had come like gunfire. I don't like being put in the defensive role.

'Because I'm a nosey-parker,' I shot at him. 'I don't like mysteries. It wasn't so I could burgle her apartment in peace, if that's what you're thinking.'

'There was no sign of a break-in,' he said. 'Whoever got in used keys. You had a set.'

'So did the concierge. So you've got at least two suspects, haven't you?'

I couldn't resist it, but I thought as I said it that it might be a mistake. He looked as if he could get very nasty.

'We checked the apartment for fingerprints,' he said. 'We found yours in just about every room.'

'That's not exactly surprising, under the circumstances.'

He paused for a moment and stared at me levelly. Then he said: 'I don't think you quite realize the position you're in. From the evidence, we could make out quite a good case that you turned the place over yourself and then raised the alarm.'

'Why on earth should I?'

'You tell me.'

'Listen,' I said, 'I've been going in and out for days to feed that blasted cat. I've had plenty of opportunity to burgle the flat without calling any attention to myself at all. What's more, I'll bet you found several other sets of prints besides mine. The concierge's, for example, and her husband's. The woman next door's. And Ann Wilcox's. Why aren't you in England interviewing her?'

'Who's Ann Wilcox?' he interrupted, frowning.

'She's the person who dragged me into this in the first place. She'd been feeding the cat for two weeks before I ever came on the scene.'

'Oh yes,' he said consideringly. 'I saw the letter.'

There was another pause. Then he said: 'What's her address in England?'

'I don't know.'

'I thought she was a friend of yours?'

37

'I only knew her for three days. She comes from some-where near Swindon. Her boyfriend too.'

'What's his name?'

'Nigel something. I don't know the surname. The temp agency might know. They might have a forwarding address too – they'll have to send her payslips on. But there's something else; there must be at least one other set of keys: Connie's own. What was taken, anyway?'

He walked over to the open window, which was still smeared with cleaning fluid.

'Jewellery, silver, video recorder, some valuable china. As far as we can tell, anyway. There was an inventory among her papers. But of course we don't know if there was any money in the place, or cheques.' He paused, then said: 'You don't mind if I look round your apartment?'

My mouth fell open. I felt myself go hot with anger.

'Have you got a warrant?' I demanded.

His expression didn't change. 'No. But I can get one if I have to. That'll take time and trouble. For everyone.'

For a hint, it was verging on a threat. I had no difficulty guessing for whom it would make the most trouble.

'Search if you want,' I said tersely. 'I've got nothing to hide.'

I finished my window-cleaning while he did the search. He was very quick and efficient, but I was fuming. I don't like the idea of strange men going through my knicker drawer.

'Find anything?' I asked, when he'd finished.

He looked at me with the eyes of officialdom: chilly, rather arrogant.

'It may surprise you to hear that I didn't expect to,' he said. 'It was a mere formality.'

'And you don't need warrants for mere formalities,' I said, pushing my luck. 'So why are you here?'

'Your name kept coming up,' he said. 'It's difficult to miss.'

I can take aggression, but I don't like it. It makes me get aggressive too.

'Have you traced Connie yet?' I asked.

'That's our business.'

'That means you haven't, I suppose?'

He wouldn't rise. Instead he snapped. 'Where do you think she is?'

This was like ping-pong. I made a decision.

'OK,' I said, 'I'll show you mine if you show me yours.'

This brought absolutely no reaction whatever. He simply waited. I pulled all the data together in my mind.

'Connie went to Italy, spent two weeks at the Villa Rosa in Florence, then departed to catch the overnight train for Brussels two weeks ago. She apparently hasn't been heard of since. Her office and her sister in England have no idea where she is. I don't know whether she got back to Brussels or not because I haven't the resources to interview sleeping-car attendants and taxi-drivers and so on.'

'We do,' he said. 'She got back to Brussels all right. The attendant on the train remembered her. But none of the taxi-drivers seem to. We've checked all the firms who were operating at the station that night.'

'Did she use her own car?' I asked, my mind racing.

He shook his head. 'It's still in her garage.' He was watching me intently.

'She could have taken the métro,' I pursued, thinking aloud, 'Or been picked up by a friend. There'd be no way of knowing.'

'The sleeping-car attendant saw her talking to a young man as she was leaving the train. About twenty, medium height, fair hair. They were speaking English. Sounds familiar to you?'

I shook my head. 'It could have been someone she met on the train.'

'It could have,' he agreed.

'Have you checked the hospitals?'

He nodded. 'Nothing.'

'So where does that leave us?'

Our exchange had been quickfire. Now he paused again and stared at me down his nose.

'It doesn't leave *you* anywhere,' he said coldly. 'It leaves *me* with a lot of work to do. You keep out of it from now on. We don't need amateurs messing around.'

Thank heaven, he was going. I did nothing to stop him. But on the threshold, he turned and said: 'I take it there's nothing you'd like to add to your statement? No useful bits of evidence you've forgotten to mention?'

His voice was so sarcastic that I lost my cool completely.

'No, there isn't,' I said angrily. 'But maybe you'd better take the cat in for questioning. With a bit of luck, she might confess.'

I expected a curt reaction. Instead, he suddenly became perfectly still, standing with his hand on the doorknob, his eyes like chips of blue slate. There was so much menace in his stillness that I suddenly felt a qualm. But damn it all, who did he think he was? I put my chin up and stared back.

He didn't prolong the encounter. Very quietly, he said: 'Don't get smart with me, Miss Haycastle,' and then he left.

At least he'd got the name right.

A moment later, I heard the sound of an engine and the squeal of tyres. They all think they have to drive like Starsky and Hutch.

I won't say that the temptation to let the police handle the problem wasn't strong. After all, he was right; it was their job. Also, whatever his manners were like, he was obviously nobody's fool. But being ordered about makes me bloody-minded. I wasn't sure that I was ready to drop the matter. I thought it over all weekend and when the phone rang on Sunday afternoon, I'd just about made my mind up. It was Connie's sister, very embarrassed.

'I don't know quite how to explain this,' she said, 'but you left me your number and I wondered if you might be able to help me. The police have rung up to ask about Connie.'

'I know,' I said, 'they've talked to me too. Listen, I've got a sort of apology to make. I don't really know Connie at all; when I called you the other day, I already knew she was missing – at least, she hadn't come home and I was trying to find out where she might be. I didn't say anything because I didn't want to alarm you.'

'But who are you, then?' Bewilderment was plain in the voice.

I explained the whole convoluted matter. There was a silence at the other end. Then Linda said: 'I just don't know what to do. I'd come over, but the baby's due next week and I can't travel like this, and David's away on business.'

'I don't think either of you would be able to do anything, anyway,' I said, trying to sound reassuring. 'The police seem to have the matter well in hand.'

There was another silence. When Linda's voice came again, it sounded as if she were asking a question that she would have given anything to avoid.

'What do you think has happened to Connie?'

'I don't know,' I said. 'But I'm damned well going to find out. That is, if you haven't got any objections?'

Linda's voice rang with relief.

'Oh no, no objections at all, it would be such a relief to know that somebody's doing something... but I surely can't impose on you to such an extent. You must have work, responsibilities...'

'Nothing that matters,' I said, and it was true.

'I don't know how to thank you,' Linda said, and I could tell by her voice that she was near to tears. 'I've been so worried. You don't know how grateful I am.'

'Well, stop worrying,' I said. 'You can help by telling me something about Connie. Does she have a regular man friend, or anyone she went out with at all?'

'Not as far as we know,' Linda answered. She sounded uncomfortable. 'The trouble is that we haven't really seen an awful lot of Connie since we got married. She and David don't get on very well. She came to visit us a couple of times but they irritated one another so much that we... well, I'm afraid we stopped inviting her. We've really rather lost touch a bit.'

'You and Connie were very close before?'

'Yes,' she said with a sigh, 'but it all changes, doesn't it,

41

when you get married. I felt – I still feel bad about it, but there wasn't anything I could do to make them like one another. Connie thinks David's a wimp and that our life's boring and suburban; and he resents it, of course.'

'Do you write?'

'Christmas cards and the odd letter. We phone from time to time, too. The last time was a month or so ago. We talked about the office; she's been having trouble with another girl who works for the same company.'

What was this? 'What kind of trouble?' I asked.

'Well, the other girl's jealous and she seems to be trying to get Connie fired. She wrote this long memo to her boss telling all sorts of lies about Connie, and Connie found out and there was a hair-pulling session. It sounded pretty horrific.'

'What kind of lies?'

'That Connie'd been having an affair with her previous boss and that's how she got the job; stuff like that. It was ridiculous; Connie's first boss was about seventy; he should have retired years ago. He was forced to, in the end. But that's all irrelevant, I suppose. The point is that this woman made it all up. She sounds absolutely deranged. Connie was fearfully upset and I don't blame her.'

'Nor do I,' I said. 'I've met the woman. But tell me something else. Who is Mick?'

Linda sounded startled. 'Mick?' she said. 'Oh, that was ages ago. Mick Taylor. They met at college and had one of those half-on, half-off relationships that never go any-where. He was a nice boy, but Connie didn't want to get tied down.'

'He went to Australia?' I prompted, listening carefully.

'He got a postgrad scholarship to go out there and then just sort of stayed on. He loved it. He came back here in the mid-eighties and he and Connie had a final fling. He wanted her to go back with him, but she wouldn't, so that was that. I always thought Connie really missed her chance there, but she didn't want to give up her life in Brussels to go and live in the outback. Anyway, he's still living out there, on a farm somewhere, I think.'

'So Connie doesn't have much reason to go back home now?'

Again the sigh. 'Not since Mum died. That was just after our wedding. We don't really have any close relatives and our friends have all died or moved away. Then when the house was sold, that was the end of it, I suppose. I don't think Connie's got any old school or college friends left here either; you lose touch, don't you, especially if you live abroad.'

We talked a bit longer, but there wasn't much else Linda could tell me and we rang off soon afterwards. I was thoughtful for a long time. That explained the gaps in Connie's photograph album. You don't take pictures when you're miserable. The first gap came after Mick's final departure for Australia. Connie had taken a while to get over that one. The life she hadn't wanted to give up must have seemed rather empty, that winter. Then Linda's wedding: a double disappointment, for Connie had lost a sister and gained an unwanted brother-in-law. I remembered the tired, rather bitter look on Connie's face in the wedding photographs. And then the final blow: the mother dying, the last ties with home and childhood cut for good. Connie was on her own.

I reflected bitterly on the 'troubles in the office' that Linda had mentioned. That only confirmed my own impression of Karin. So she wanted Connie fired? Might she have been desperate enough to do something drastic about it? In any case, what hell on earth life in that office must have been. The dreadful thing was that this particular situation wasn't all that much out of the ordinary. People die by inches in offices, eke out their lives in atmospheres of spite and hatred and bigotry, afraid to lose the small security they possess by looking for something new, or else too miserably aware of their own shortcomings to risk changing.

If the police thought I was going to give up on this now, they had another thought coming.

Chapter 6

As I've said before, Brussels bristles with English-language amateur dramatic societies. It's an old truism that whenever two Brits get together abroad, they set up a theatre group. Here, the Americans, the Irish and the music-lovers do it too, and if you've got any talent at all (and a surprising number of people do), you can participate in a variety of productions ranging from the *Messiah* to *The Relapse* and *The Tempest*, taking in *Guys and Dolls* and *Translations* on the way.

I thought it might take a while to infiltrate the theatre crowd, because they're less active in the summer; but a quick zip through the local English language press informed me that there was a club night that Tuesday at one of the Brussels cultural centres. It was a movement workshop, followed by a play-reading, led by a rather handsome lady in late middle age, who spoke in the assured, well-rounded tones of one who had been on the professional stage in her youth.

The session wasn't particularly well attended; there was a hard-core of club members, who all knew each other very well, and two or three newcomers, including me. The average age was mid-twenties to thirties, so I didn't feel too much like a lemon, although I have trouble keeping a straight face when asked to pretend to be a falling leaf. The play-reading was more fun: they did bits from *The Importance of Being Earnest* and I got to read Gwendolen, who is a delicious bitch.

Afterwards we all went down the road to the local café for a drink, and my patience was rewarded, because the one topic of conversation round the circle was Connie. The news had got out already. I shouldn't have been surprised, because Brussels is a small town if you belong to the English-speaking community, and it's full of interlocking circles, so that everybody knows everybody else, though sometimes indirectly. Connie had disappeared, and they couldn't get off the subject.

'What I can't understand is that Connie's such a quiet, sensible person. She's the last person to come to a sticky end.'

'What makes you think she has?' I asked, startled.

The speaker, a fat, lively girl with round brown eyes, waved her hands in the air as if to negate her remark and said hurriedly: 'I don't! I just mean that she's the last person you think *would*. *If* she has. Which I'm sure she hasn't.' She had read Lady Bracknell with a great deal of talent earlier on.

'What do you think has happened, then?' I asked, trying to keep my tone conversational.

'Haven't a clue!' the fat girl said.

'Well, Connie's a dear, dear friend of mine,' said a young man opposite me, 'and if you ask me, she's run off to Rio de Janeiro with some delicious young man.'

He was fairish, of medium height and very slim: casually, but very carefully dressed. He moved with beautiful precision; I'd noticed him during the movement workshop and had been impressed; he alone had managed to convince me that he was a falling leaf. He had a round little face which was full of sparkling malicious merriment when he talked; in repose, however, all his features drooped in a melancholy way. His voice was light and rather affected, with a barely suppressed Birmingham accent. He stared at me with wide-open brown eyes, gauging the effect of his remark.

'Does she know any delicious young men?' I asked lightly.

The fat girl gave a loud hoot of laughter.

'Connie? You must be joking, Phil. One of the lads, old Connie. Half a pint of shandy down the pub after the

45

game.' There was barely concealed contempt in her voice.

'That's all *you* know,' Phil retorted, looking rather put out. He took a cigarette out of his little zip-up bag and lit it pettishly.

'Good squash player, though,' the fat, noisy girl, Frankie, went on. 'You can always rely on Connie if you want a partner.'

'Doesn't she have a boyfriend or anything?' I asked innocently. I looked at Phil as I said this, but he'd obviously decided he wasn't going to play any more, for he sat back, crossed one knee over the other, and smoked his cigarette, staring into the distance, the elbow of his right arm supported by his left hand.

Frankie gave another contemptuous, chimpanzee-like hoot.

'Not on your life. Connie's quite happy with her cat. Sign of an old maid, having a cat. Shows you've given up hope.'

'Maybe she just likes cats?' I suggested.

Someone else said: 'What's happened to Hortense, anyway?'

I confessed that I was looking after Hortense, because I was a friend of Connie's sister in England. They swallowed that, to my relief, though I noticed that Phil suddenly looked quickly at me again, rather furtively.

The evening broke up without my learning anything more. We all parted, with many reminders from Frankie that there was another session at the same time next week. The night was warm and peaceful, out of the busy chatter of the café and well away from Frankie's jungle noises. The summer weather was holding well. Warm nights are a luxury in these northern climes and it seemed a pity to go to bed, so I drove into the centre of town and went for a stroll in the Grand'Place. It's always breathtakingly beautiful at night, with the ornate baroque façades and gold decorations glowing in the floodlights. Tonight the lovely old guild-houses were hung all around with silken banners in bright colours; people strolled to and fro across the cobbles, their voices hushed by the

46

height and grandeur of the buildings. The sight of beauty always calms me down.

I had a disagreeable task to do the next day, so I went to get it over with straight away. I was waiting outside Sundsvall International the next morning at eight o'clock when Karin arrived. I stepped out of my car as she approached the front door and she saw me and stopped with a jerk, suddenly white as a sheet of paper.

'What do you want?' she said. Her voice was almost a hiss.

'Just a word,' I said. 'Connie's sister told me you've been trying to get Connie fired. I just wondered what the police would say if I told them that.'

For a moment, I thought she was going to hit me. Her face became all screwed up with anger. She clutched her handbag fiercely to her body.

'Think you'd better tell me if you know anything,' I said.

'I have nothing to tell you,' she snapped. 'You have no right to come here harassing me. You are like your precious Connie: a liar. You should go away. I shall call the police. You are a criminal.'

Her voice was shrill with hysteria, and a few passersby glanced at us strangely, but no one interfered. You could die on some of these streets and no one would do anything, but I guess that's the same in any big city.

I'd thought that perhaps I might catch Karin off guard and shock her into admitting something, but it looked as if I'd misjudged the situation completely. I was dealing with someone quite incapable of rationality. She hated Connie too much. You can't do anything with irrational people, because they don't listen. I wasn't going to get anything more out of Karin. She pushed her way through the glass doors of the building and disappeared into the gloom, leaving me outside reflecting on my lack of psychological delicacy.

I had my own job to go to, not too far from the Avenue Louise, as it happened. It was a one-man office; the guy was out most of the day selling that fancy French glass that looks like china, and wanted someone to sit and answer the phone. His secretary was on holiday. I couldn't think what she did with herself all day long. The average daily number of phone calls was around six, including wrong numbers, with occasional interest in the form of the postman bringing up registered letters, or the window-cleaners coming by. I got so bored that I cleared up six months' backlog of filing and ended up dusting the china in the showroom, just for a change.

In between, I rang up various friends in the Commission and found out that Connie had worked there for eighteen months, not in a Directorate General because she was over the age limit, but on one of the special projects that mushroom in fertile Community ground, something to do with international computing standards, rejoicing in the name of PICTS. She'd worked for a Dutchman who had later moved on to Luxembourg, then for several other bosses, and she'd left PICTS three years ago to go to the job at Sundsvall. She'd applied to have her PICTS contract extended, but the application had been turned down. She'd also applied for other jobs in various Commission projects, but equally without success.

I then took my courage in both hands to ring Sundsvall and ask the name of Robinson's predecessor. I dreaded hearing Karin's voice, but in the event, an unfamiliar man answered the phone; it was Jarnstedt and he gave me the information without demur. The name was Patrick Bennett, and he had retired and gone back to the UK the previous year. So that was that. I hadn't the resources to start combing the UK for retired gentlemen called Bennett. It was back to my only viable lead: the theatrical set.

There was nothing on except a musical soirée of Gilbert and Sullivan songs, performed in a rather beautiful *hôtel de maître* on the Avenue des Arts. I consider Gilbert and Sullivan to be the musical equivalent of tiddlywinks, but the performers put a lot into it and some of them could even sing. However, I was glad when the interval came. I elbowed my way though the crush at the bar to get a glass of champagne and then retired with my back to the wall to contemplate the throng. They all knew one another and the room rang with shrill theatrical intercourse. I marvelled anew at some people's ability to maintain a conversation while never ceasing to search the crowd for someone more interesting to talk to.

A voice said: 'Well, hello. How's Hortense?'

I recognized the precise tones. It was Phil. With him was a sulky blond boy with a carefully trained lock of hair falling over his forehead and a gold ear-ring. The blond boy said: '*Mais c'est qui, celle-là?*' and Phil said: '*Une amie,*' and smiled at me.

'Hortense is fine,' I replied. 'Do you like cats?'

'I adore them,' he said. 'I've got one myself. Are you enjoying the show?'

'It's OK,' I said cautiously.

'There was the most terrible scene backstage before curtain-up,' Phil said with relish. 'I thought Melissa and Deirdre were actually going to come to blows. Amateur sopranos all think they're Jessye Norman.'

'I thought she was a tennis player,' I said.

His whole face seemed to twinkle.

'Is there any more news about Connie?' he asked.

'I haven't heard any,' I answered. 'Have you?'

'Why should I have?' he countered lightly. The blond boy, who evidently didn't understand English, shrugged and moved off into the crowd, where he was instantly absorbed.

'It was just your comment about Connie going off to Rio de Janeiro,' I said. 'You seem to know her rather well.'

'Yes, well, Connie likes gay men,' Phil said. The brown eyes had the wide measuring look again. 'She understands our problems. I suppose it's because she has the same problems herself.'

What was this? He was trailing his coat but I had no idea how far he was prepared to pursue it. It wasn't exactly the place for private revelations. We were surrounded by gesticulating people in evening dress, roaring at one another.

49

I said incredulously: 'Are you saying that Connie was a lesbian?'

I'll swear his crack of laughter was genuine: I'd surprised him into honesty.

'Good heavens, no!' he said. 'Connie liked them young, casual and as straight as possible, if you'll pardon the expression. She liked screwing ski-instructors and waiters on holiday, that sort of thing. Away fixtures.'

'Don't we all, if we get the chance?' I said, wisecracking automatically and meaninglessly, because I was struggling to fit this news in with the ladylike image I had of Connie.

Phil laughed again and said: 'You stole my line.' Then he added: 'Though there was that gorgeous Australian who came over. An old friend, she said. I wish I had old friends like that.'

'But that was in eighty-five,' I said, frowning. 'If you mean Mick, that is.'

'That's the one, but it wasn't in eighty-five,' Phil said. 'I didn't know Connie then. He was here a month or two ago. He stayed with her for a few days and she brought him to a show.'

'A month or two ago!' I repeated stupidly.

'Well, you know what Antipodeans are like,' Phil said, a touch of tolerant scorn in his voice. 'Come over for six months with no money and hitch round Europe sponging off friends and relatives.'

'Is he still here?'

'No. He's gone off to Germany or somewhere. And he was talking about going to Eastern Europe after that. But he's coming back here before he goes home to his sheep farm, because he's got another friend here he wants to see. Wish it was me.'

'Do you know the friend's name?'

'Tom Lister. Lives in Schaerbeek,' he said. He stared at me very intently. 'Listen, when I said gays and women have the same problems, I meant that we're after the same things and afraid of the same things, so we understand one another. And we've got a common enemy.'

'Men?' I said.

He nodded.

'We're after love,' he said, and his little face became melancholy. His eyes wandered over the crowd, searching maybe for his blond friend. 'We're afraid of getting old and ugly and dying alone. We want romance and glamour and living happily ever after.'

'Is that what Connie wants?' I asked. Any minute now the blessed bell was going to ring for the end of the interval.

'Of course she does,' he said. 'She thinks she's found it now, too. Only she's being led up the garden path, like all those other stupid cows.'

The malicious look was back on his face.

'Mick?' I asked.

He laughed again. 'Oh no. Somebody much more important. But it's a secret. Nobody knows but me.' He was like a teasing little boy dangling a tempting toy in front of another kid.

'Shall I tell you about it?' he said, maddeningly.

But I was nearly there myself now. There's only one reason for keeping an affair secret in this town. These stories always turn out to be frighteningly banal.

'Let me guess,' I said. 'She's having an affair with a married man? So tell me something new.'

He abandoned his game suddenly, looking disappointed and rather petulant. 'You're really hard-boiled, aren't you?' he said rather bitterly. 'You don't look it, but you are. I bet the guys go for you in droves. I hope you treat them like garbage.'

'What's his name?' I asked.

The bell rang, ear-splittingly. It was an old school dinner-bell, wielded by a young punk in a dinner-jacket. It made my teeth ache. Phil made to move away, under cover of the noise, but I grabbed his arm and yelled my question in his ear a second time.

'I don't know his name,' he said, snatching himself away. 'Connie never told me.'

He plunged into the tide of people swirling back into the concert room and was swept away from me. I stayed put, anchored to my wall, my empty glass in my hand.

Later, sitting in my flat with Hortense purring like a little machine on my lap, I pondered on the obviousness of it. The expatriate community is overloaded with single women: au pairs, secretaries, eager young graduates doing a stint at the Commission, female executives in multinational companies. But most expatriate men are married, many of them with wives back home. It's very easy to slip into a relationship with an attractive man whose wife is away. You don't have to think about it too much; you get carried away with the romance and daring and it's only later, when you're sitting in your flat alone while he's home with the wife and kids, that you start to realize what you've got yourself into. It's a guaranteed recipe for loneliness. At first the times together make up for the holidays on your own, the opportunities you miss because you're waiting for the phone to ring, the potential lovers you turn off for his sake, but after a while you've got to be very good at self-deception not to realize you've marooned yourself and sunk the lifeboat. And Connie had fallen for it, like so many before her.

I stroked Hortense, marvelling at the dynamic force pent up in cats. How is it possible for such a small, fragile body to contain such life? I could feel her heart beating quickly under my hand; and yet this cat was a match for Fu Manchu himself. I felt myself becoming tender towards Hortense, but she sensed it, looked up with a short sound of enquiry, and then bit my hand sharply. Nothing lasts.

Chapter 7

I rang Tom Lister, who turned out to be a Scotsman with one of those soft Highland accents that sound like singing. He couldn't have been more helpful. He readily agreed to ask Mick to call me on his return to Brussels, though he, Lister, wasn't quite sure when that would be. In the next two or three weeks, perhaps. I had to be content with that. I just hoped Lister would remember. It's so easy to lose a phone message.

The weekend came again. Saturday morning was hot and sullen. I put on my garage mechanic's clothes and went down into the street to perform an operation on my car. One of the best things I ever did was to take a course in automobile maintenance: if ever there was a way to meet men, that's it, and you learn a lot about cars too. To the great amusement of passers-by, I was eventually obliged to get underneath the vehicle. Pairs of feet on the ends of assorted legs went briskly to and fro; a dachshund stopped to sniff at my front wheel and I addressed an uncomplimentary epithet to it, which it returned in spades. Then I noticed that a pair of feet had assumed a stationary posture on the pavement by my side. A pair of brown leather men's shoes, large size. Lightweight beige trousers. Hell and damnation. I stuck my head out.

'Nothing to do down at the nick?' I said.

Luc Vanderauwera was definitely not looking friendly. I doubted whether he ever could. He said: 'Get out of there,' and it was not a request. I debated for a moment, then wriggled out and stood up. I was not looking my best, but there was no reason to be bad-mannered. I said: 'Good morning, Inspector. How are you?'

53

I might as well have kept my mouth shut. He said: 'I want to talk to you. Inside.'

He sounded very, very angry, and I had a fleeting thought that I might be safer in the street. He must have read it on my face, because he said tersely: 'It's all the same to me, but I'm sure you'd prefer your neighbours not to hear this.'

I was beginning to get angry myself now. What damn right did this objectionable man have to boss me about? I led the way in without a word, taking the stairs so as to avoid getting in the lift with him. Once in the flat, I put the width of the dining table between us and faced him.

'Well?'

He said: 'What does it take to stop you interfering?'

'Death,' I answered. 'What's your problem now?'

'Everywhere I go, you've been there first. I thought I told you to stay out of this.'

'All I've done is talk to people and there's no law against that.'

'You talked to Karin Andersen?'

'I tried.'

'And thanks to you she's in a clinic with a so-called nervous breakdown and we can't get in to interview her through the wall of medical certificates.'

'A nervous breakdown?' I repeated, startled.

'After her interview with you, she apparently collapsed in hysterics and had to be taken off in an ambulance. Her doctor says she has to have complete rest for several weeks.'

'How very convenient,' I said, my anger rising steadily. 'That way you can't get to ask her why she hated Connie Trevor so much she was prepared to lie about her in order to get her fired. What else was she prepared to do to get rid of Connie?'

'We'll never know now, will we, thanks to you.' In the stress of anger, a trace of an accent was noticeable in his English. 'I'll tell you this just one more time. Stay out of it. If you don't, we'll find a way to make you.'

'What with?' I said. 'A truncheon?'

We stared at one another, both of us white with temper. The phone rang, startlingly. I grabbed the receiver and snapped 'Yes,' and a young man's voice said: 'Lebrun. *Police Judiciaire.* Is Inspector Vanderauwera there?'

'Yes. He's here. Do you want to speak to him?'

'No, no need,' the voice said, rather hastily. 'Would you mind telling him his wife called? She wants him to call home. An emergency.'

'OK,' I said. I wasn't in the mood to be polite. I put the phone down and passed on the message, somewhat brusquely.

Vanderauwera looked at his watch, muttered something under his breath, and pushed his hair back in the first uncontrolled gesture I'd seen him make. There was a short silence. I looked at his face and knew exactly what he was thinking. He needed to use the phone and he was too damn proud to ask.

Hell, let men be stiff-necked if they want to be. I said: 'You can use my phone if you want.'

'I'll pay for the call,' he said, giving me that look down his nose.

'If it makes you feel better, you can pay for the call,' I said.

I left him to it and went to the bathroom to clean up. I looked a mess. Out in the living room, I could hear Vanderauwera's voice rising in exasperation. At least I wasn't the only one he shouted at. He was speaking French. From the snatches I heard, I gathered it was something to do with picking up a child from a football game. The conversation reached a crescendo and ended with the sound of the phone slamming down. I went out again. He was standing in the middle of the room, looking tired and angry. Hortense was sitting interestedly on the table beside the phone.

I get these compassionate impulses from time to time. I said: 'Would you like some coffee?'

For the first time, he looked nearly human. He said: 'Thanks, no, I've got to go and pick up my son.' He took a twenty-franc piece out of his pocket and put it down on the table. He seemed to have run out of conversation.

I said: 'Did you know that Connie was having an affair with a married man?'

It was obviously news to him.

'How do you know?' he asked.

'One of her theatrical friends told me. A guy called Phil.'

'The little fag?' he said scornfully.

I might have known he'd turn out to be a homophobe as well. However, it was hardly the time to go into the semantics of homosexuality. I repeated patiently: 'He told me that Connie was having an affair with a married man.'

'I talked to him too,' Vanderauwera said obstinately. 'He didn't mention it to me. What's the man's name?'

'Phil didn't know.'

He gave a sudden derisive laugh. 'Is that what he told you? Everything except the name?'

I felt myself flushing. 'We were in the middle of a concert. I could hardly beat it out of him.'

'Well, I can,' Vanderauwera said.

'You do that and I'll report you,' I said between my teeth.

I could tell from his face that he knew I meant it. He didn't flinch.

'And you know what'll happen to your report?' he asked, and made the contemptuous gesture of dropping something into the waste-paper basket.

I said: 'I have friends in the Ministry of the Interior.'

It's true. I do. One, at least.

Vanderauwera paused and gave me a measuring look.

'And the press,' I said. 'French and Flemish.'

He folded his arms and looked at me calculatingly.

'Listen,' he said. 'You want to find out who this guy is, don't you? Well, from my wide experience among the reptiles of Brussels, I'll bet you a million francs that your Phil won't tell us anything unless we put pressure on him.'

I had to admit that he was probably right.

'So what kind of pressure would you find acceptable?' he asked.

It was a good question.

'Can't we try just asking him?' I said.

'Oh, we can try,' Vanderauwera replied. 'At least, you can try, since you're determined to do my job for me. I'll watch. Then we'll see how far you'll go to get what you want. Or is that too much for you?'

I looked him in the eye and said: 'When?'

'Tonight. I'll pick you up when I come off duty. Around eight.'

He seemed to be in a suspiciously good humour as he marched out of the apartment, and I had a fleeting thought that I'd landed myself right in it this time.

I was quite right. It turned out to be one of the worst nights of my life.

To start with, he was two hours late. It was past ten when the curt ring on the doorbell sounded. I'd already written off the evening and was in no conciliatory mood. He was waiting in an unmarked police car down below. I suppose it was stupid of me to expect him to apologize. Instead he said: 'I've got the address. We'll go round.'

His car looked as if it had had a hard life. It was fitted with radio equipment, which emitted a soft crackle from time to time. The seat-belt on my side was broken. His looked OK, but he hadn't bothered to fasten it. We crossed town without speaking. He drove expertly, but terrifyingly fast and with total disregard for the car. We finished up in a quiet street outside a pretty, newly reno-vated town-house with geraniums at the windows.

There was no answer to the doorbell and no lights were on in the house. Nobody at home.

'What now?' I asked suspiciously. I was beginning to wonder if this might be a set-up.

'Saturday night,' Vanderauwera said. 'He's probably out partying. We'll do the rounds.'

'What rounds?'

He turned towards me and there was a look of derisive satisfaction on his face. 'The gay clubs,' he said. 'Or don't you have the bottle, Miss Haycastle?'

Needling brings out the worst in me. I folded my arms and stared at him with all the contempt I could muster. School playground stuff. Well, it always used to work in those days.

'Try me,' I said.

One day I'll learn to keep my mouth shut.

I'm not a party-goer by nature. I hate night-clubs and discos and noise and cigarette smoke and beautiful people trying to get off with one another. I hate the shrillness, the brittleness, the desperate stupidity of it all. That night as we went from one dark thunderous cavern to another, I saw everything that makes me want to go and build a cabin on some mountain and stay there for ever. In one place they were having a fancy-dress evening, and I felt as if I'd got into one of those awful distorting mirror places and couldn't get out again. We weren't exactly popular once they realized what we were about. People jostled us and threw filthy looks at us. I heard venomous mutters of '*Sale flic!*' aimed at Vanderauwera and worse things whispered at me.

Vanderauwera marched through it all like a man wading through a swamp with a flame-thrower, his undisguised contempt scorching out a path for him. I envied him his untouchability. I felt sick. Despite all my brave words, I felt contaminated. When we stood on the pavement again among the ordinary crowds coming out of the late-night cinemas on to the Toison d'Or, I felt as if the air in my lungs would never be clean again. We hadn't found Phil. But I'd long ago realized that that wasn't the point of the exercise. I was being chastised.

It was raining now, and all the neon lights were flashing in the raindrops and on the glistening pavement. The town is beautiful at night, in the rain. Vanderauwera turned to me, his face unreadable.

'Had enough?' he asked.

The bastard. But I can be pig-headed too, when I want to.

'No,' I said grittily. 'Not till I find him. We'll try his house again. If you're feeling tired, I can always take a taxi.'

That got him. I saw his face tighten, and felt a hot surge of satisfaction. He turned and led the way back to the car without a word. It was parked illegally and had acquired a ticket, which he tore up into confetti and dropped in the gutter. I was too tired even to yawn as we rocketed across town again. Outside Phil's house, Vanderauwera leaned on the doorbell until lights began to go on all up and down the street. It was three in the morning. I was shivering.

Phil opened the door, bleary-eyed. Behind him, as at the concert, hovered a beautiful boy, but this was not the sulky blond of the other night; this one had a fine, dark gazelle's face with brown eyes and a frightened expression.

Vanderauwera said: 'Police,' and shoved his way in, flashing his official card briefly and throwing a curt 'Come on!' to me over his shoulder. As the door closed behind me, the gazelle disappeared up the stairs in a quick flurry of movement. A door slammed somewhere in the house.

Phil said: 'What do you want?'

Vanderauwera went right through into the living room, just as he'd done in my flat. It must be a technique they learn in police school. There was a dining table with a sandwich and cup of tea on it. A late snack after a night out, I guessed. Phil was dressed in tight black trousers and a fringed black shirt with lots of fancy detail on it. He looked tired and dry-skinned. His eyes were red-rimmed in the rather harsh light, and his hair looked dull. I don't suppose any of us looked a picture. Even Vanderauwera's face was marked; the night had left black traces around his eyes and in the hollows under his cheekbones.

Phil turned to me and said with venom: 'So you go for big brutes of policemen, do you? And I thought you were such a nice girl!' He pulled a chair out with a defiant gesture and sat, staring up at Vanderauwera and reaching at the same time for his cigarettes and lighter, which were on the table.

Vanderauwera waited till Phil was lifting the lighter, then, casually, he plucked the unlit cigarette from between the other's lips and tossed it away. Phil jerked backwards, dropping the lighter, and for a moment he looked like a small snarling animal. I opened my mouth to protest and then shut it, grimly. There was no choice but to see this through now. What was another layer of muck after this night?

'Go on, big boy, beat me up,' Phil said, though Vanderauwera hadn't touched him at all. Phil's manner was a mixture of defiance and fear, but there was something else there which I needed a moment to identify. Then I saw it. It was provocativeness. He wanted Vanderauwera to lose control. He was hoping for violence.

'The lady wants to ask you something,' Vanderauwera said. As in my flat, he didn't raise his voice. He didn't need to. His stillness was menace enough.

Phil glanced sideways at me. They both waited.

I suddenly felt like the question-master on *Mastermind*. I cleared my throat. How should I put it? Who is screwing Connie?

'What is the name of the married man with whom Connie is having an affair?' I said. Top marks for grammar, Matilda. My voice sounded hoarse with tiredness.

'I don't know,' said Phil. 'And even if I did, I wouldn't tell you.'

Vanderauwera moved very slightly, and Phil's eyes flicked back to him, half-fearfully, half-anticipatively.

'Of course you know,' Vanderauwera said measuringly. 'You know all the gossip. Who, when, how, why – all the dirt on your friends' little affairs. Your kind always does.'

'What do you know about my kind?' Phil said, lifting his upper lip. The animal peeped out again briefly, something small with a pink nose and sharp white teeth.

'More than I want to,' Vanderauwera replied. Distaste was plain on his face. 'What's the name?'

'Go on, make me tell,' said Phil softly. The look in his eyes was almost feminine, but not quite. I felt the same distaste that I could see on Vanderauwera's face. Phil turned to me as if he could sense it, needling.

'Do you get off on seeing him beat up gays? I bet

you like being knocked about yourself, don't you? Tough women always do.'

I was too tired; control slipped away for a moment. 'For Christ's sake,' I cried out, 'Connie's your friend! Don't you care what's happened to her?'

He answered, his own voice shrill with tension: 'Why should I? I've got enough problems of my own!'

'Tell us the name,' Vanderauwera said again. His voice alone had remained calm, and it shocked both Phil and me, so that we turned and looked at him. Phil's face changed to an expression that was both sparkling and sly. 'What will you give me for it?' he said. I think he was enjoying himself.

Vanderauwera said: 'Fetch your friend down and let's have a look at his papers.'

There was a long, long silence, while the excitement slipped out of Phil's face and left him looking tired and worn. When he spoke, his voice was scarcely audible.

'You always find a way, don't you?' he said wearily.

Vanderauwera said: 'The name, and anything else you know.'

'If I tell you, will you leave Ahmed alone?'

'Yes,' Vanderauwera said. His face was expressionless. Phil made us wait for it.

'Graham Ferguson,' he said, after a long pause. 'He's English. A Eurocrat, or at least, he was, but he's left the Commission now. Connie met him when she was working on PICTS and it was *Gone With the Wind* and *Doctor Zhivago* all rolled into one, poor cow. He told her he'd get a divorce as soon as the kids grew up, but if he ever does, I'm the Flying Dutchman. No good telling Connie, of course. Women are all the same; only hear what they want to.' He shot me a malicious glance.

'He got her the job at Sundsvall?' I asked. Phil nodded.

'He twisted some guy's arm – an old guy who owed him a favour. Her contract with PICTS had run out.'

'Where's he working now?' Vanderauwera asked.

'He was offered a partnership in a consulting firm with a couple of other guys and they're making millions.' Phil sounded terribly weary. 'They're big wheels in the artistic world – sponsorships and all that.'

'And Connie's still seeing him?' I asked.

'I don't know,' Phil said, closing his eyes. 'You'd better go and ask him yourself, hadn't you?'

There it was; the result of our night's work. We'd got what we wanted, but I suddenly thought of the filth we'd had to wade through, and fury overwhelmed me. I made an abrupt movement and Phil sat up fearfully in his chair, while behind him, Vanderauwera looked suddenly up at me, his eyes almost black with fatigue. But I was well away by then.

'You rotten little creep,' I said, hearing my voice shake. 'So Connie's a dear, dear friend of yours, is she?' I heard myself mimicking him crudely and saw him flush. 'You don't give a tinker's damn whether she's dead or alive! You won't even help when you're asked. You sit here smirking and playing sick moronic little games. What the hell does the word "friend" mean to you anyway?'

Phil was stung into replying. 'Who do you think you are, dear, Joan of effing Arc with a flaming sword?' he said between gritted teeth. 'Nobody asked you to stick your big nose in. Why don't you pack up your holy purity and wheel it out of my house? We like our air sullied in here.'

There was no answer to that, so I turned on my heel and marched out, flinging open the front door and getting out into the fresh air again with unbearable relief. I was shaking so much that I had to lean against the car. Behind me, Vanderauwera closed the front door of the house. He unlocked the car and said curtly: 'Get in,' and I let fly, unable to take any more. 'Go boil your head,' I said. 'I'll get home on my own.'

Grabbing my handbag firmly, I set off up the street with the dogged determination of the very drunk or the very tired. It was a one-way street and the car was facing the other way. Behind me, I heard the door slam, the engine start and the car move off into the distance.

It was a long street and before I got to the other end,

I'd had time to realize that it was four in the morning, that there were no trams or buses around, and that the chances of getting a taxi in that part of town were non-existent.

Then as I turned the corner, I saw the car standing by the kerb with Vanderauwera beside it. He'd driven round the block to head me off. I stopped short and we stood facing one another for a moment. A dog barked somewhere. Holding open the passenger door, Vanderauwera said quietly: 'It's late. Please get in.'

I was too tired to argue. I got in, leaned back and closed my eyes. I don't remember much about the drive home. My mind was in free-fall. I do remember that I suddenly asked, out of the blue: 'How come you speak such good English?' and he replied, quite normally, as if we hadn't been snapping and snarling at each other ever since we'd met: 'My mother's English. I used to spend the school holidays with my grandparents in Petts Wood.'

Then there was silence again until the car stopped. There seemed to be nothing to say, so I got out and went into my apartment block. It took ages to get the key into the lock. As I turned to lock the glass doors behind me, I saw that the car was still standing in the road. I wondered what he was waiting for, but I was too tired to pursue the thought.

Upstairs, Hortense paused for a moment in her nocturnal gymnastics, checked me in, and resumed her silent leaping from armchair to sofa to table. I headed for the bathroom, stood under the shower until I felt I couldn't stand up a moment longer, then staggered to the bed and fell on it, wet hair and all. As the pit swallowed me up, I thought I heard a car start up down below, but I couldn't be sure and by then I really couldn't have cared.

Chapter 8

I don't remember much about Sunday. I slept for most of it. When I finally dragged myself out of bed, I felt the way you do after a major operation. I suppose ninety-nine sensible people out of a hundred would have given up after the previous night. But I'm the hundredth idiot. If Vanderauwera had intended to teach me a lesson, he'd failed. Monday, I had a new job to start and by then I'd decided on my next move. It was time to call in the Man from the Ministry.

Georges Duchanel is my highest level Belgian contact. He's very rich, very eccentric, and comes from one of eighty or so families who run Belgium. That means he knows everyone who is anyone. Georges is my opera-going friend. We met because our season-ticket seats at the Opera adjoin. Georges lent me his handkerchief during a particularly emotional moment in *Parsifal* and our relationship has never looked back. He made a few dutiful but half-hearted attempts at gallantry in the beginning, but seemed thoroughly relieved when I politely indicated that I wasn't interested. We also share a taste for good wines, although Georges pretends I have no refinement because I prefer Chassagne-Montrachet to Puligny-Montrachet. But, as I keep telling him, nobody's perfect.

Georges is around forty-five, but pretends to be much older. He's very tall and rather overweight, and is always exquisitely dressed in a rather old-fashioned way: he likes fancy waistcoats and silver-handled canes and that sort of thing. He is balding and wears a pointed beard. His face inspires confidence. There is a decided twinkle in his eye.

Why he works in the Ministry of the Interior is a total mystery to me, as he doesn't actually need the money, which is just as well, considering the pitiful salaries Belgian civil servants earn. But Georges likes to have his fingers in lots of pies. He lives in an incredibly beautiful flat in the Galéries Royales, full of genuine Empire furniture, with a manservant to look after him in the best English style. He keeps an elegant, middle-aged mistress in an equally elegant town-house, which she shares with her aged mother. He visits her twice a week. I find myself totally unable to imagine what they get up to.

Georges has a couple of rather bizarre characteristics. One is that he is absolutely fascinated by the art of warfare, or indeed, anything military. Napoleon is one of his heroes, which makes for interesting discussions, since Wellington is one of mine. Georges has a whole room lined with books on battles, tactics, weapons, fortifications and the like. He knows it all, from the Hundred Years War right up to the conflict in the Gulf.

Alongside this characteristic is a macabre and disconcerting sense of humour. Georges loves to say things which embarrass people to death, and he has a huge laugh which could drown out the London Philharmonic. I was once privileged to see him bring a dinner party to its knees.

The dozen or so guests were English, American and French, of the concerned liberal persuasion, and the conversation got round to the horrors of the Second World War. Georges was sitting next to a dark, earnest woman who was leaning much too close to him, as people do when they're short-sighted and too vain to wear glasses, grinding on and on about the terrible, terrible things that had happened in the concentration camps. After listening for some minutes with an expression of the most devoted attention, Georges said: 'Ah, yes, yes, terrible, Madame, terrible. I lost a relative myself in a concentration camp.'

The dark lady was all gushing sympathy, and Georges let her run on for a while before heaving a huge sigh and saying: 'Indeed, yes. It was a very sad thing. He fell out of his watch-tower.' And then his huge booming laugh rolled round the table, while the dark lady and the other guests recoiled in horror and the hostess's face froze. It cost Georges a fortune in conciliatory flowers the next day, but he reckoned it was worth it.

'I do not like having my – what is that expression you use, Matilda? – my ear bent by earnest people who think they know more than I do. It was a boring party. People should keep their distance.'

For the first time in weeks, I was busy at work, that Monday. My new assignment was in a small, bustling office run by an energetic and competent Israeli entrepreneur whose secretary had broken her ankle falling off a tram. It was a sharp, well-run team, and for once, I found myself so caught up by the work that I reached the end of the day without having had time to call Georges to arrange a meeting. I got home late and hungry; we'd only had a sandwich lunch because of all the meetings. I was still jet-lagged from Saturday night. I called Georges and arranged to see him the following evening, then went to bed to try and catch up on my sleep. I'd need my wits about me the following day.

I was glad I'd done it, too, because Tuesday was another all-day meeting. My new boss, Aaron Silverman, asked me to take verbatim notes, and then to summarize the proceedings for the company after each break, and believe me, that takes some concentration. By the end of the afternoon, I was nearly worn out. As we were clearing up, Aaron said: 'That was a good day's work, Matilda,' and I was ridiculously pleased. It's nice to be considered competent by the competent.

I was late for my appointment with Georges and arrived hot and dishevelled. As ever, the sight of a greeny-gold Burgundy bottle and a plate of salmon canapés had a most strengthening effect. Georges greeted me with four kisses, two on each cheek, which is a particular ritual of his. 'Beautiful as ever,' he declared, which was gallant of him, because I wasn't. 'I could make neither head nor tail of what you said on the telephone, Matilda, so you will have to begin again, from the beginning.'

I went through the story, in between heart-strengthening sips of the best white wine in the world: Connie's failure to return, the burgled apartment, Karin Andersen's suspicious behaviour, Vanderauwera's attitude and now this news about Graham Ferguson. Georges listened with a frown of concentration on his face. Finally, he said: 'But what do you wish me to do, Matilda?'

'I want to meet Graham Ferguson and I thought you could help.'

'May I ask why? What will it achieve?'

'I want to see his face. I want to find out what he knows.'

'But why not leave it to the police? This Inspector of yours will certainly make investigations. Why interfere?'

I thought for a moment. 'Two reasons. Firstly, I'm pissed off at being treated like a complete imbecile by this Vanderauwera. But mostly, it's because I feel I owe it to Connie. I don't think the police really care tuppence what's happened to her. She's just another name on a list to them. Do you know Ferguson?'

Georges stroked his beard, still frowning. 'Yes, I do. He is a patron of the arts, like myself. But if there was an illicit affair, he will not wish to answer questions about it. There are the wife, the family, the business connections to consider.'

'Tough,' I said, very shortly. 'I'll be discreet.'

'You are interfering in people's lives.'

'He interfered in Connie's.'

'Matilda, I do not understand you,' Georges said sadly. 'You have the face and body of a young dryad, and the soul of a Vandal. You upset me.'

'Listen, Georges,' I said. 'Connie's a single woman over the age of forty. Nobody's bothered. Nobody cares except one bad-tempered cat, the sister in England, and me. That strikes me as a sorry state of affairs. How would you like it if you disappeared and nobody gave a damn where you'd gone?'

'It would be a refreshing change,' Georges said with faint irony. 'Have you thought that maybe she does not want to be found? Perhaps she wishes to start a new life.'

'She'd have made arrangements about Hortense,' I said. 'Connie wouldn't have left her. Everything else, maybe, but not Hortense. Nothing will make me believe that. Will you help me, Georges?'

Georges looked at me reflectively and said: 'Of course. I just wanted to make sure that you knew what you were doing.'

'How can I meet Ferguson?'

'Ah. Drink your wine, Matilda, and I shall ponder.'

Georges ponders best to music. I allowed myself to be overwhelmed by *Turandot*, while my veins gradually filled up with liquid gold, and Georges pondered. Music and wine together have a strange effect on me; I was beginning to feel as if I were growing roots when Georges leapt up, stopped the CD player in the middle of 'In Questa Reggia', and announced:

'I have a plan.'

'Spill the beans,' I said.

'Ferguson and his wife are founder-members of an artistic society called "Cultura". It is a non-profit-making organization which supports young European performers and artists; all very laudable and politically correct, and contributors obtain not inconsiderable tax relief on the side. Many wealthy Belgians are members.'

Did I also mention that Georges is a cynic?

He went on: 'I believe they have a grant from the EC, but they also make quite reasonable sums of money from their activities. They organize exhibitions, concerts and other cultural manifestations and they have a high media profile.'

'Sounds interesting,' I remarked.

'On Friday, there is a cocktail at the Palais des Beaux-Arts to celebrate the opening of a new exhibition of Belgian Post-Impressionists. The Royal Family is rumoured to be attending. The Fergusons have probably received an invitation. I shall check. If they have not, I shall arrange it. They will certainly go, and you and I shall go too. I shall introduce you. After that, it will be up to you. Do you have a suitable dress?'

'Of course,' I said indignantly. 'Even Vandals have cocktail dresses these days.'

'Sexy?' Georges enquired, with a lift of his eyebrows.

'Very,' I said firmly.

'Good,' Georges said, looking satisfied. 'You will vamp him, and I shall watch.'

Chapter 9

The week went by so fast that I hardly had time to turn round. By Wednesday, I felt I'd been working in that office all my life. I was part of the team. It was an unaccustomed feeling, and I enjoyed it. We were designing and installing added-value computer systems to the small and medium-sized businesses who can't afford IBM, and things were humming. They were a nice bunch of people: a couple of Israelis, a couple of Dutchmen, one American, an Irish girl, and me.

Aaron Silverman looked like everyone's idea of a hero of the Six Day War, although he was just young enough to have missed it. He was big and dark and bronzed: a whole millenium away from the little black-coated and black-hatted men who run the diamond community in Antwerp. His energy voltage was staggering. He was one of those people who go to bed at two in the morning and leap out again bright and fresh at six. He was exhilarating and exhausting to work with, and we all did our utmost for him. I almost felt guilty about leaving the office on Friday afternoon, even though we were all coming in on Saturday so as to get a presentation ready by Monday morning. My mind was still busy with slides as I got ready for the cocktail party on Friday evening.

My dressing-up routine takes forty minutes from start to finish, including bath. I put on a little black dress which cost more per square inch than any other garment I possess, and took some trouble with my make-up. Georges's eyes positively gleamed when I joined him in the foyer of the apartment building.

The Palais des Beaux-Arts was packed out with big ladies like sequinned walls and languid young men in unstructured suits and pony-tails. There were lots of traffic policemen creating chaos outside; inside, we had to fight through a mob of press people and TV cameras. Georges steered me through by my elbow, while I did my impression of Brigitte Bardot at the Cannes film festival. The people were wall-to-wall. Half of them seemed to be waiters. I hadn't the faintest idea where to start, but Georges is used to this kind of thing. Unerringly, his nose turned towards the place where the important people were gathered. Nodding and smiling majestically at acquaintances, still clutching my elbow possessively, he manoeuvred me through the throng, stopping to introduce me to one or two beaming old buffers who kissed my hand, while I kept the starry-eyed smile pinned to my face.

An extra flurry in the crowd and increased noise outside informed us that the Royal Family had arrived: I couldn't see who it was, but Georges informed me that it was Prince Philippe, and he seemed to know. A knot of people moved through the cordon into the exhibition, with a tall fair young man in the middle – the Royal party. The rest of us had to wait a while, which wasn't too hard, considering there was enough champagne around to float the Sixth Fleet. Finally, just as my feet were beginning to tell me they'd had enough, down came the cordon and in we went.

I read later in the papers that it was a good exhibition. I wouldn't know. Georges and I dashed through it like a pair of road-runners and emerged breathless at the other end to be greeted by yet more waiters with champagne. Georges looked round, his nose up like a pachyderm scenting water, and said: 'Aha!'

'Where?'

'In the corner, under the potted palm.'

'Which one is he?'

'The one with the reddish hair.'

I saw a clutch of fashionable people smiling and chatting together, champagne glasses in their hands. They all smelled of Money with a capital M. My quarry was the tallest. He was in his early forties and he dominated the others, not just because of the height advantage, but because of a certain arrogant confidence. He had broad shoulders set off by a well-cut dinner-jacket, a reddish complexion, and dark auburn hair, expensively cut. There was a playful smile on his face; he was telling a joke, judging by his hand gestures and the anticipatory looks of the people round him. The punch-line came as we watched and they all roared with laughter. Ferguson gazed round the room in that smug way people have when they've told a good one, caught sight of Georges and lifted a hand to wave a greeting.

'Come on,' Georges said, seizing my elbow.

The group opened up as we approached and Ferguson held his hand out.

'Georges, my old son! Where on earth have you been hiding yourself? Haven't seen you for ages.'

There was just a hint of the industrialized north of England in the voice, but you had to be sharp to catch it. Glassy blue eyes turned on me with a look of appreciation.

'And who might this charming young lady be? Introduce us, Georges old boy, introduce us.'

Smiling benevolently, Georges introduced me all round.

You can tell a lot about people by the way they shake hands. Graham Ferguson shook mine lingeringly, the appreciative smile still on his lips. His hand was large and thick-fingered and carried a heavy gold signet ring. His wife gave me a warm quick handclasp and a genuinely friendly smile. Her name was Vibeke. Scandinavian, I thought. My guess was confirmed by her perfect skin and natural shiny fair hair; she looked as if she'd spent her life bathing in pure Nordic springs.

Georges moved rapidly on to a Belgian couple whose lengthy name I failed to catch. The husband, grebe-like with tufted hair and black and white clothes, lifted my hand jerkily to his lips, just stopping short in the formal Belgian manner which always makes me want to giggle. Madame was so lacquered and made-up she looked like an extraterrestrial. She barely condescended to touch my fingers with her own cold hand.

The third couple had an English name which I also instantly forgot. He was dark, with a pleasant smile and a warm, firm handshake. She was taller and fair-haired; her expression was snooty and her handshake cursory in the extreme. A distinct whiff of stale cigarette smoke emanated from her. I resisted the temptation to wipe my palm on my frock, and turned my attention back to Graham Ferguson. He hadn't taken his eyes off me all the while. I had the distinct impression I'd been reviewed, summed up, docketed, and was about to be winkled out of my shell.

'You don't have a drink,' he said. He summoned a hovering waiter with a lofty snap of the fingers, took a glass of champagne off his tray and handed it to me. Thanks for asking what I wanted, mister. As it happens, I like champagne, but I was tempted to ask for lemonade and see what his reaction was.

'What did you think of the pictures?' he asked, smiling down at me.

I tried with difficulty to remember what the pictures had been like.

'Well, to be honest,' I said, 'I prefer the Impressionists myself. What did you think?'

'Not much,' he said. 'Where I come from, pictures are something you hang up to hide the stains on the wallpaper.'

He looked at me expectantly. I recognize a ploy when I hear one.

'Really? Where do you come from?' I asked obediently.

'The Far North. Bradford.' He pronounced it Bratford, to add, I suppose, a deliberate touch of authenticity. 'Mills, mines and working men's clubs. A bit of a far cry from all this.' He waved his hand at the chattering beau monde around us.

'Oh, I don't know,' I said innocently. 'Ilkley's pretty exclusive, if I remember rightly, and that's just up the road from Bradford, isn't it?'

He paused and looked at me for a moment. I guessed

73

that he was trying to decide whether I was daring to poke fun or whether I was just as thick as two short planks. At that moment, the dark-haired man spoke laughingly.

'Graham's the most determined philistine I know,' he said. 'It's no good asking his opinion about anything cultural. He only comes to these things because it's good company policy.'

'Well, some of us didn't have the benefit of a public-school education,' Ferguson said. There was a smile on his lips, but it didn't go up as far as his eyes. 'And there are compensations. Meeting lovely lasses, for instance.' He turned to me again, having obviously decided for the two short planks. 'I must say, old Georges is a man of surprises. You're not his usual style at all. Not that I'm criticizing his taste, you understand.'

Georges, deep in conversation with the Belgian elements in the party, was out of earshot. I wondered briefly what his usual style was. I searched for a suitable cliché and found one without too much difficulty.

'Georges and I are just good friends,' I said. 'We go to the opera together.'

'I understand entirely,' Ferguson said. 'Been in Brussels long?'

This is the standard opening move in the eternal game of 'Let's get to know one another'. I hate playing games, but if I was going to find out anything, I'd have to go along, like it or not. 'Seven years. How about you?'

'Four or five. Seems like for ever,' he said. 'Can't say I like it much, but the money's good. But it's not like the UK, is it?'

'No,' I said.

'Can't get a decent British banger anywhere. Still, at least we've got the BBC – don't feel completely cut off from civilization.'

The British expatriate community in any sizeable foreign town inevitably harbours a few dinosaurs who still believe that Britannia rules the waves and wogs start at Dover. They come in all shapes and sizes, but they have one thing in common: an IQ which would disgrace an amoeba. I wondered if Ferguson's attitude was genuine and decided it couldn't be. He was obviously a clever man, lack of public-school education or no. Furthermore, he was watching me carefully to gauge what effect he was having. Playing games turned him on. I've met men like that before. They're a total waste of space. However, I had business with this particular specimen. Persevere, Matilda.

'Having the BBC can be a mixed blessing,' I said.

The dark man laughed. 'I couldn't agree more.'

'Don't cut in, Julian old son,' Ferguson said, a touch patronizingly. 'This young lady and I are just getting to know one another.'

'You can't keep her all to yourself,' the other replied mildly. 'Though I don't blame you for trying.'

He had a cultured voice with a hint of laughter in it. I looked at him properly for the first time. He was about the same age as Ferguson. He wasn't madly good-looking and his evening clothes looked as if they'd been around a while, but there was a twinkle in the grey eyes and he had those child's eyelashes that are always so enticing on grown men. I smiled back.

'I'm sorry,' I said, 'but I didn't catch your name.'

'I'm not surprised, the way Georges rattled it off. It's Julian Wychell. I'm Graham's business partner.'

'Oh yes,' I said.

'And at the risk of being too cultured for Graham, I must say I thought the exhibition was extremely impressive. I particularly liked the van Rysselberghes myself.'

'I agree with you about the exhibition,' I said. 'But which were the van Rysselberghes?'

We talked about the pictures for a minute or two and then got on to art in general. It was very pleasant, but unfortunately if Julian Wychell had actually wanted to cut Ferguson out of the conversation, he couldn't have found a better way to do it. Ferguson's eyes glazed over; after a few minutes he lost interest and drifted away. At least the indifference over art wasn't feigned. But all the same, drat!

The dark man smiled at me. 'Graham overdoes the

Room at the Top bit,' he observed. 'But he's a really good chap. We've been partners for a couple of years now and I've got to know him well.'

'I'm sure you're right,' I said. 'Tell me who those other people are. I didn't catch their names either.'

'The tall fair lady is my wife Françoise, and the couple Georges is talking to are the Baron and Baroness de Ligny-Meeûs. That's not as grand as it sounds. Belgium's bursting at the seams with minor nobility, as I'm sure you know. Barons and baronesses are ten a penny.'

'And the ancestral châteaux all have leaky roofs. I know,' I said. 'Your wife's Belgian too?'

He nodded, smiling.

'She owns an art gallery downtown. Hence our interest in this kind of thing. Tell me, do you like very modern art?'

'It depends,' I said with some caution, for I have had my views on modern art contested before now. Haphazard heaps of sand or motor-car innards don't constitute art as far as I'm concerned.

'Well, I admit there's a lot of poor work about,' Wychell said, 'but you shouldn't let that put you off. Some people are doing really good things. For example, the society I belong to is putting on an exhibition by an excellent young Belgian painter. It's at my wife's gallery next week. Why don't you come along and extend your knowledge? The *vernissage* is on Sunday and we'd love to see you there.'

'I'd love to come,' I said. 'But tell me more about this society. Who belongs to it?'

This sounded really useful. If I could get a foot in the society's door, I might have a chance to get at Ferguson more easily.

Wychell seemed only too delighted to explain. 'It's called "Cultura" and all sorts of people belong. The Fergusons, for example, and the Ligny-Meeûses. My wife's family. Your friend Georges. Anybody who feels they can devote either some of their income or some of their time. Even my daughter condescends to lend a hand now and then, which is some condescension from a teenager today, I can tell you.'

'Are the Fergusons helping with the exhibition on Sunday?' I asked, hoping it sounded casual.

'Indeed they are. We couldn't get on without Vibeke. She's a dynamo of energy.'

'Well,' I said, thinking rapidly, 'couldn't I do something to help too? I'd love to get involved.'

'Of course,' he said, beaming. 'We can always use a willing pair of hands. But I ought to warn you – it won't necessarily be anything glamorous. It might be handing out drinks, or even doing the washing-up.'

'That's OK,' I said, smiling. 'I'm a great washer-up. Where and when?'

He was writing down the details on the back of a business card when I became aware that Georges was at my elbow. Julian Wychell looked up.

'I'm just roping Miss Haycastle in for Françoise's exhibition,' he said. 'You wouldn't like to help too, would you, Georges?'

'Alas,' Georges said, with seemingly genuine regret, 'I shall be unavailable that day.'

Wychell said nothing, but his smile deepened somewhat. He obviously knew Georges well.

The party was breaking up, and we left soon after that. I hadn't had a chance to get near Ferguson again. Georges's maroon Bentley was parked on a yellow line outside the Beaux-Arts and a policeman was hovering worriedly around it, not sure whether it was official or not. Georges waved him away and handed me in gallantly. I looked down at the business card in my hand. The name of the firm was De Jonckheere, Ferguson and Wychell, European Legal Consultants, with an address in the Avenue de Cortenbergh. In pencil on the other side was written: Sunday, 17.00h., Galérie Rimbaud, with an address near the Grand-Sablon.

'Well?' said Georges.

'Not a lot of progress,' I replied. 'I didn't get to talk to Ferguson much, but I'm helping out with the *vernissage*

77

on Sunday so I may get a chance to collar him then.'

'The pictures will be unspeakable,' Georges said. 'What did you think of Ferguson?'

'I'm not sure. He's not what I expected at all. I liked his wife, though.'

'You certainly seemed to be enjoying Julian's company,' Georges remarked slyly.

'Yes, I did,' I said. 'He's a very nice man. Who's De Jonckheere?'

'Julian's brother-in-law. He put up the money and provides the connections. Julian and Ferguson do all the work.'

'Are they doing well?'

Georges looked at me cynically. 'What do you think? Explaining the ramifications of Community law to the bewildered masses of the business community – it is a bottomless market. A goldmine.'

I found I was looking forward to Sunday. In the meanwhile, though, there was still Saturday to come.

Chapter 10

Working Saturdays is not something I like to do often, but I have to admit that I enjoyed the next day. You can get far more done when the phone isn't ringing every two seconds. Aaron and I worked well together. I like a man who knows his own mind. At six-thirty, the presentation was finished and Aaron offered to buy us all dinner. Two or three spouses were telephoned in haste and joined us at the restaurant. It was a great evening. They were all about my age, multinational, well travelled, intelligent, fun. I felt at home, which doesn't happen very often.

Aaron, who to my surprise was unmarried and apparently unattached, ended up sitting next to me. He had a great line in lengthy hilarious Jewish jokes. We didn't leave the restaurant till nearly midnight. Our table was the last to go home and the waiters were getting the Hoovers out and setting the places for tomorrow as we finally made our rather merry exit.

I slept late on Sunday, in preparation for the *vernissage*. A *vernissage*, I should explain, is a cocktail party held to celebrate the opening of a new artistic event, to which the in-crowd flocks, done up in its best new togs, to see and be seen. Some people will do anything for a glass of champagne and a baked prune wrapped in bacon.

The Grand-Sablon is one of the most beautiful squares in Brussels, and today the sun was bright on the lovely church with its stained-glass windows, the ornate Flemish façades of the houses and the antique shops full of tempting and expensive objects. There were crowds of people sitting out in the pavement cafés eating, drinking, chatting and enjoying the lovely summer weather. The dealers from the Sunday morning antiques market were still folding up their striped awnings and packing up their unsold stock into vans and cars.

Parking round the Sablon is about as easy as climbing the North Wall of the Eiger. I managed it in the end, but had to walk some distance back to the gallery. It was five o'clock on the nose when I got there. It was a small gallery, but exceedingly select. Georges had been right about the pictures. They were in the pointillist style and rather large; you couldn't really get far enough away to admire them properly. Ghent might have been far enough. Close up they looked like large clumps of pastel-coloured dots. I'd have Monet, myself, if I could afford it.

A little silvery bell rang as I pushed the door open. A number of people were already there. Several faces turned, and one I recognized detached itself and came towards me. Vibeke Ferguson, radiant with health and goodwill.

'Julian said you'd be along,' she said, smiling warmly. 'How nice of you to come and help. We thought you could hand out leaflets to people as they arrive. Come on, I'll show you round and then introduce you to everyone.'

Her voice sounded like a small stream running over pebbles. She took me round the gallery, chattering happily away. At the back of the gallery was a *bijou* loo, a kitchen the size of a hamster-cage, and a glass door leading out into a paved garden enclosed by whitewashed walls. Hanging baskets of fuchsias and red geraniums lent a Mediterranean air. A couple of tables were set out, with bright parasols leaning over them.

Three young ladies were sitting at one of the tables, looking the picture of fed-upness. Two of them were teenagers, one fair, one dark, both pretty. They were wearing the standard summer uniform of frayed blue jeans and cut-off cotton T-shirts straining over adolescent podge. They evidently shared a hairdresser, for their long hair was in an identical Renaissance crimp. Both had an air of haughty fifteen-year-old sophistication.

The other girl was in her late twenties and she'd been working on her sophistication for years. She was wearing a cream pleated skirt and a rose-pink silk top embroidered with pearls and silver thread. It looked lovely; she was built like a girl-child with almost no curves at all. I'd have looked like a ceremonial elephant in it. Her brown-fair hair was long and thick, held back by tortoiseshell combs. She had a small polished face with wide-open blue eyes, a pursed mouth and arched eyebrows that gave her a weary, bored look. The look intensified considerably as Vibeke and I approached.

'My daughter Imogen and her friend Clare,' Vibeke said, indicating the teenagers. 'And this is Isabelle Lefèvre, another intrepid volunteer. Matilda's come to help us out today. Now I'll leave you all together to get acquainted. I have to sort a few things out before the Ambassador arrives.'

I was left facing a hostile and suspicious silence. Six eyes flicked over me, summing up the quality of my clothes, my social standing, and my form as a competitor in the sex-appeal stakes. I failed on the first two counts. Imogen and Clare looked at one another briefly, with the merest touch of sneering contempt, and looked away again. Isabelle turned her elegant little head and started to study her glossily enamelled nails. I could just about forgive the brats; they were still wet behind the ears. Isabelle was something else. She was old enough to know better. No, on second thoughts, she'd probably never be old enough to know better.

Apparently none of the young ladies were conversationalists. 'Nice weather we're having,' I said, and they all stared as if I were bonkers. I was just about to ask if they'd read any good books lately when Graham Ferguson appeared in the glass doorway.

'Anyone for drinks?' he enquired. Then he saw me, and a pleased smile spread over his face.

'Why, it's Georges's little protégée,' he said. 'Melanie, isn't it?'

'Matilda,' I said, suppressing irritation.

'Nice to see you again. Drink?'

'Why not?' I said.

'Come into my parlour,' he invited, with a gallant sweep of his arm.

The blonde nymphet said repressively: 'Dad, you know Mum said we weren't to have drinks *before* the exhibition.'

Ferguson raised his eyebrows. 'What Mum doesn't know won't hurt her, will it?' he said, and disappeared inside.

I followed him into the kitchen. He'd been unpacking wine-glasses. The stainless-steel draining board was crowded with them. The small space was restricted even further by crates of wine and soft drinks stacked in one corner. At the sink, Ferguson turned and beamed at me.

'And what can I get for such a lovely lass?' he asked.

'What's on offer?' I asked.

'Well, that's a leading question.' His eyes wandered boldly down to my chest. 'Pretty dress,' he said.

He'd be asking if I had a bra on next. I frowned. 'Kir, if you have it,' I said briskly. 'White wine, if you don't.'

'I've got anything you want,' he said, smiling. 'One kir coming up.'

He knew how to make a kir properly. He poured the cassis first and then the white wine, with an air of considerable professionalism.

'You've worked behind a bar,' I observed.

'In my youth,' he said. 'Holiday jobs. Didn't have a rich papa like some people. I was hoping I'd see you again. Thought we might have an opportunity to get better acquainted. Unless you think Georges would mind?'

'I don't suppose he'd mind at all,' I said truthfully.

'Funny old bird, Georges, like all these Belgians. We do a lot of business with Belgians. A rum bunch. Never know what they're thinking. Give me the good old Anglo-Saxons every time.'

'What business are you in?' I asked.

'We're legal consultants,' he said. 'Give people advice on the legal implications of Community Directives, that sort of thing.'

'That must be difficult,' I said. 'Do you have lots of contacts in the Commission?'

Ferguson picked the drink up and advanced across the tiny kitchen towards me. I'd have backed off, but there was nowhere to go. He stopped, much too close, and looked me in the eye in a playful, knowing way.

'Yes we do,' he said. 'But that's quite enough about me. Why don't you tell me something about yourself instead? I bet a pretty girl like you can have a high old time in a town like Brussels, if you know what I mean.'

His hands were a couple of centimetres from the front of my dress. I brought both my own hands up, pushed him firmly out of my space, and took the drink from him.

'Later,' I said. 'I've got work to do.'

He didn't seem particularly put out. I don't think it even occurred to him that his attentions might be unwelcome. I went back into the gallery, perplexed. How on earth was I going to get to talk to him about Connie? All he seemed to want to talk about was me.

The Three Stooges had also come back in. The last thing I wanted to do was go over and join them. Fortunately, the door opened just then to admit Julian and Françoise Wychell. Immediately there was a stir. Vibeke bustled over to them, Graham Ferguson appeared in the kitchen doorway, and the dark girl said in a more normal fifteen-year-old voice: 'There's Mummy and Daddy.' Even Isabelle lost her air of boredom and seemed to perk up.

Vibeke came over to us, staggering under a cardboard box full of printed leaflets. She dumped it on a chair with an 'Ouf!' of relief.

'Hot from the press,' she said. 'And only just in time, as usual. Imogen, I think your father needs some help in the kitchen.'

The blonde nymph's face fell. 'Oh, Mum!' she said. 'Can't we do something more interesting?'

'Imogen, I won't tell you again,' Vibeke said, her voice firm. The nymphs trailed off with much pouting and tossing of hair, the picture of unwillingness.

'Teenagers!' Vibeke said to Isabelle and me. 'They may look grown-up but take it from me, they're just little children underneath. Mind the print on the leaflets – it smears. Now, I'd better tell you what you have to do. Oh my goodness, is that the time?'

Our job was to collar people at the door and hand out the leaflets, which gave a synopsis of the painter's career so far (which took up a line and a half) and a description of the works on show, with prices. The prices made me blink.

'How many people are you expecting?' I asked, looking at the box, which seemed to contain about a million leaflets. Julian Wychell followed my gaze and laughed.

'Yes,' he said. 'We did go rather over the top. But I expect Vibeke's invited the entire Scandinavian colony of Brussels, haven't you, Vib?'

'I most certainly have,' she said firmly. 'And they'd better come, or I'll want to know why. The Ambassador promised he'd be here by six-thirty. He has a dinner afterwards, so he can't stay long.'

'Is the painter here himself?' I asked, curious.

'In the corner with Françoise.'

I looked. He was a pale twitchy young man with John Lennon specs, and he didn't look at all well. He was drinking coffee with shaking hands.

'It looks as if he's got first-night nerves,' I observed.

Rather unfortunately, I have a voice which carries. Françoise Wychell heard me and glanced up with her usual haughty expression. She caught my eye, and I smiled politely and nodded. To my surprise and discomfiture, she ignored me completely, reached into her bag for a cigarette, lit it, and blew out a long puff of smoke. I felt my ears getting hot. That kind of superior bad manners gives me a pain in the brisket. I hoped she'd taken out fire insurance.

People were starting to come in. Wychell glanced around at them, then at his watch and said: 'Do you all know what to do? Good. You'll have to excuse me for a few minutes. I've got a phone call to make before the rush begins. I'll be upstairs if anyone needs me.'

He headed off towards a spiral flight of stairs in one

corner, which I hadn't observed before. There must be an office up above.

'To work,' Vibeke said. 'Leave the Ambassador to me, when he arrives. He's rather shy.'

I seized a handful of leaflets and stationed myself near the door. A large bunch of people came in, all talking Swedish, and surrounded me. Isabelle seemed to have disappeared. I was busy handing out leaflets when I heard a sort of hiss behind me, and someone said: 'You!'

I turned, startled, and found myself face to face with Karin Andersen.

Oh dear, oh dear, oh dear.

She was white to the gills and all clenched up with tension.

'What are you doing here?' she said, still in that hissing voice. 'You are persecuting me. You are following me everywhere I go!'

I gaped, unable to think of anything to say. People were beginning to turn, their faces surprised.

'Why don't you just leave me alone!' Karin's voice was rising. 'I am not well. I cannot be treated like this.'

I saw Vibeke appear at the kitchen door, followed by her husband. She came hurrying over, her face concerned.

'Why, Karin, what is all this?' she said. 'What's the matter?'

'This woman is persecuting me. She came to the office and told lies about me to the police and now here she is again. Everywhere I go, she follows me.'

She seemed to remember she was speaking to a countrywoman then, for she burst into long tirade in Swedish. Around me the Swedes nodded and muttered darkly.

In the midst of my horrified embarrassment, I had time to feel a fleeting pity for the poor artist sitting forgotten in a corner, his pictures abandoned. The spectators were all gravitating towards the live show, which was much more interesting. Vibeke listened concernedly to the tirade, which ended in a flood of tears, then turned to me and said anxiously:

85

'Is this true? You denounced Karin to the police?'

'No, it's not true,' I said. 'The police have been making enquiries about someone we both know – a girl called Connie Trevor who works with Karin.'

'Connie Trevor!'

The exclamation came from Graham Ferguson, and we all turned to look at him. Karin lifted a ravaged face and cried out: 'Yes, Connie, your precious secretary Connie. I hate her! I hate her! I wish I had never seen her.'

I exclaimed, startled: 'Connie was your secretary?'

A voice said: 'What on earth's going on here?'

It was Julian Wychell, standing at the foot of the stairs with Isabelle just behind him. Vibeke said, relief and appeal in her voice: 'Oh, Julian, Karin's not well. Please come and help. We must take her home.'

'I am perfectly well,' Karin announced, blowing her nose fiercely. 'It is this woman's fault. She will not leave me alone.'

'I didn't even know you were coming here!' I protested. 'How could I?'

Julian Wychell took command, in a quiet authoritative way.

'Vibeke, will you see Karin home? I'll take care of the Ambassador when he comes. That's a good girl. Graham and Matilda, come on upstairs to the office. Isabelle, would you mind keeping an eye on things down here for a minute or two? Ladies and gentlemen, please help yourselves to drinks. There are refreshments out in the garden, too.'

Upstairs in the office, he said: 'Now, Matilda, what was that all about?'

'Karin and I have both been involved in a police enquiry about the disappearance of a girl called Connie Trevor. She works in the same office as Karin and they don't get on. Karin seems to have got it into her head that I'm persecuting her.' That left out a lot, but it was basically the truth. I added: 'I had no idea Connie'd been Graham's secretary.'

'She wasn't my secretary for long,' Graham interrupted

angrily. 'She couldn't handle the job and we didn't renew her contract.' His face was red and his whole manner full of an odd mixture of resentment and unease.

'Did you know she'd disappeared?' Wychell asked, looking at him.

Ferguson stared back, still flushed. 'The police have been round asking questions,' he said. 'I told them I hadn't seen her for three years and sent them away with a flea in their ear.'

'You should have told me,' Wychell said quietly. 'We do work together, after all.'

'I said I'd dealt with them,' Ferguson insisted, his voice rising. 'There was no need to worry you.'

'I see,' Wychell said. 'Are the police pursuing the matter?'

'I don't know, but I didn't much care for the look of the chap who interviewed me. He's a troublemaker if ever I saw one.'

'It must be the same one that spoke to me,' I said wryly. 'Was the name Vanderauwera?'

'Something like that.'

'He's been talking to all Connie's friends and colleagues,' I said reassuringly. 'It's a real nuisance, but I'm sure it's just the usual routine. I wouldn't worry.'

Ferguson looked a little less rattled at that, to my relief. The last thing I wanted was him taking fright at the whole business. Or finding out that my presence was more than mere coincidence.

'Well, we'll just have to leave the matter there and see what transpires,' Wychell said. 'But let me know if the police call again, Graham, there's a good chap. And would you mind leaving us alone for a couple of minutes? I'd like a private word with Matilda.'

As Ferguson's steps echoed down the stairs, Wychell looked at me with a slight twinkle and said: 'Well, this hasn't turned out to be such a pleasant experience for you as I'd hoped. I am sorry.'

'It's not your fault,' I said. 'Nobody knew Karin was going to turn up.'

'Well, I hope it hasn't put you off. Can I take it you're still interested in helping us out in the future?'

'Definitely.'

'Good. There's a concert coming up next weekend. Are you on?'

'I am,' I said, smiling.

'I'm glad to hear it.'

The dark-haired nymphet met us at the foot of the stairs.

'Mummy said to tell you that she's taken Jean-Claude home. He's got one of his headaches. And the Ambassador's arrived.'

Jean-Claude was the artist. A diplomatic illness if ever I saw one.

Wychell groaned. 'Oh God, that's all we need! Vibeke was going to introduce them. That was the whole point of the Ambassador coming.'

'He's a diplomat,' I said. 'He'll rise to the occasion.'

'Mummy's not very pleased,' the girl said.

'No, I don't suppose she is,' her father replied, grimacing slightly. 'Well, come on, troops. The show must go on.'

The show went on. Nobody bought any pictures. I wasn't surprised. The Swedish Ambassador did his stuff manfully and left for his dinner party. The level of conversation rose alarmingly as people began to drink in earnest. But even a light veil of alcohol couldn't help the paintings. Vibeke reappeared shortly before the end of the *vernissage*, having taken Karin home and put her to bed with a tranquillizer.

The punters had all gone on elsewhere by half-past nine. Wychell and Ferguson were clearing up the debris, while Vibeke and I did the washing-up. Isabelle had mysteriously disappeared, which, when I came to think about it, was entirely predictable. One look at those scarlet nails had convinced me that washing-up wasn't much in her line. The two Renaissance cherubs had gone off to a party. At the sink, I took the opportunity to mention Karin.

'I'm really sorry to have caused all that stir. It certainly wasn't intentional and I hope she's not too upset.'

'Don't worry about it,' Vibeke said reassuringly. 'Nobody blames you. We all know how highly strung Karin is. She's been having all sorts of trouble at work, you know, and that does put a strain on people.'

'What kind of trouble?' I asked, trying to sound casual.

'She thinks her bosses are trying to get rid of her, and of course, she'd never find another job with the same kind of salary. She has no real qualifications. It's very difficult for her, on her own with a child to support.'

I said nothing. Ferguson came in with a tray of glasses, winked at me behind his wife's back, and went out again. His self-confidence seemed entirely restored.

'It's a bit of a coincidence that Karin's colleague used to be your husband's secretary,' I remarked lightly.

'Well, you know what a small place Brussels is,' Vibeke replied. She had eyes the colour of gentians, and just as guileless. 'Everybody knows everybody else – it's rather alarming really. You've been a real help tonight, Matilda. I do hope we'll be seeing you again.'

'Yes, I'm helping with the concert next week.'

'Oh, I am pleased. So many people volunteer, but when it comes down to doing some real work, they vanish into thin air. Mentioning no names, of course.' She gave me a comical look and I laughed. I liked this woman. How had she ever come to marry a man like Ferguson?

As soon as I got home, I called Georges. His voice was reproachful.

'Matilda, do you know what time it is?'

'Ten-thirty. Georges, have you got any contacts in the Commission? High level, I mean.'

'Naturally. May I ask why?'

'It seems that Graham Ferguson was Connie's boss for a while. Can you find out any details?'

'I can try. May I go back to bed now?'

'Bed? It's not even dark. It's a waste of time going to bed at ten-thirty at this time of the year.'

'That's all you know,' said Georges, and rang off.

Chapter 11

It was another busy week in the office. Our hard work on Saturday paid off. The presentation went well and we got the job. On Tuesday afternoon, Aaron brought in champagne to celebrate. Afterwards, as we were all clearing our desks to go home, he stopped beside me and said: 'Mat, what would you say if I asked you to come to the cinema with me tonight?'

Yes. Of course.

We went to see the latest American serial thriller, which was moderately entertaining. Brussels is a movie-mad town. It has more cinemas per square inch than any other major city I know, plus its own film festival, and new films appear here weeks before they get to London. Furthermore, the great linguistic divide means that foreign films mercifully don't get dubbed. You get the original version with two sets of subtitles instead. Still, anything's better than bad dubbing.

After the film, we went for a drink, sitting out under the warm summer sky. I was surprised to discover that on his own with me, Aaron was quite different from his office persona, unexpectedly quiet, almost shy in fact. He told me a lot about Israel. He was born and brought up on a kibbutz and hadn't enjoyed it much. He was a great sportsman: squash, tennis, water-skiing, hang-gliding. I was impressed; my idea of sport is doing *The Times* crossword. He'd run a business in Tel Aviv for several years after university and military service. He'd been engaged to a girl there, but she'd kept postponing the marriage and had finally broken off with him.

'For career reasons,' he said, with a laugh. 'She felt

marriage would cramp her style. She's very successful now; she's a film director. So I decided to try my luck in Europe.'

He wanted to know all about me, but I'm not a great one for talking about my private life, so I skimmed over the details of my broken engagement and subsequent affairs. It's not exactly edifying, anyway. I suppose youth and inexperience can just about account for falling for a bent British copper, but I was definitely old enough to know better by the time I got to Paris. It didn't make much difference though. I suppose it never does when you fancy somebody. It took me a while to discover that Jean-Paul was a great believer in personal freedom within relationships – for himself at least. He's probably still asking himself why I left. After that I decided to settle for friendships as far as men were concerned, and I've managed to stick to it, apart from a brief fling with a visiting American journalist, who had a slow Western drawl and an irresistible way of calling me 'Ma'am'.

Three men in ten years is hardly record-breaking in this promiscuous age, but I still didn't want to tell Aaron. It was none of his business, yet. Despite the lovely weather we didn't stay out too late; we both had to work in the morning. Aaron drove me home and didn't even try and kiss me in the car, but we made another date for dinner on Friday.

He had the sense to keep his manner businesslike in the office. I was grateful; after all, I was a newcomer to the team, and didn't want to cause dissent. I know only too well how often and how quickly that can happen, and I didn't want anything to spoil this job.

Mid-week, I had a call from Vibeke Ferguson about the concert.

'Saturday night,' she said. 'A concert of Renaissance music in the Eglise des Minimes. Have you got a pencil and paper? I'll tell you how to get there. Oh, and would you mind putting up a few posters? In your office, perhaps, and anywhere else you think appropriate. I'll come round and leave them in your letter-box.'

I gave her my address and took down the details of the

concert. Renaissance music usually means krummhorns and harpsichords. I hoped they wouldn't be wearing doublet and hose and silly hats with feathers in them.

The week whizzed past. I was looking forward to my date on Friday night. This was turning out to be a great summer socially. But on Friday afternoon, I was a little taken aback when, in front of everybody in the office, Aaron casually said: 'Pick you up at seven-thirty, Mat?'

I said 'Yes', but I didn't miss the surprise on the faces around me, nor the slight pause before normal conversation resumed. I hoped they weren't thinking I was the boss's pet. Over dinner I mentioned it in passing, but Aaron only smiled.

'Don't pay any attention,' he said. 'What we do outside the office is our own business. They don't own me. It's the other way round.'

That wasn't quite the reaction I'd wanted, but I didn't press the point. We were in a wonderfully classy Italian restaurant on the Chaussée de Waterloo. Aaron had gone over the top; he'd even bought me orchids, which is old-fashioned and a waste of money, but how could I refuse? We had champagne, and it was one of the best meals of my life. I immediately promised myself a gastronomic holiday in Tuscany.

Aaron insisted on paying the bill, despite vigorous protests from me. I like to pay my share, so as to be free of obligations concerning what happens afterwards. It's difficult to say 'No' when a man's just spent a fortune putting you in the mood. But short of snatching Aaron's credit cards, there was little I could do this time. I sat clutching my orchids on the short drive home, wondering whether or not to invite Aaron up for a final *pousse-café*, or anything else. I decided against it. It had been a really romantic evening, but for some reason I didn't really feel like it. However, Aaron kissed me, briefly and rather decorously, in the foyer downstairs. He was big and solid and masculine and comfortable, and that was the way he kissed. His hands didn't even wander. Oddly enough, I was conscious of slight disappointment as I went up in the lift.

If I thought the week was busy, the weekend was a positive whirlwind. It started on Saturday morning. I was wakened by a combination of Hortense, who jumped on my head at eight o'clock, and the telephone. It was a man's voice and I didn't recognize it.

'I'm Mick Taylor,' it said. 'I got a message you wanted to talk to me.'

Mick Taylor?

Dear God, Mick Taylor!

'Yes, I do,' I said, waking up all in a hurry. 'But not on the phone. Can we meet?'

'Well, the thing is, I'm flying out today. My plane leaves for London in a couple of hours and I'm just about to go to the airport.'

'I could meet you there,' I said, thinking rapidly. 'It won't take long. I'll meet you at the British Airways desk.'

Better make sure it's the right Mick Taylor, I thought, weaving rashly in and out of taxis on the way to the airport. But I didn't have any doubts when I finally pounded into the departure area, which was packed out with long queues of charter passengers, and found him. Older, leaner and browner, but the same face as in those photos of Connie's. Long fair hair bleached even fairer by the sun. Greenish eyes. A bit of all right, in fact. I introduced myself, then we sat down in two hideously ugly and uncomfortable plastic bucket seats and got straight down to business.

'Connie?' he said, incredulous. An acquired Australian accent was there, faint but recognizable. 'What do you mean, disappeared?'

'Just that. She went on holiday to Italy, came back, and vanished. Nobody seems to know where she is. I was wondering if you had any ideas.'

'Not a clue,' he said, frowning. 'I only stayed with her a few days. It wasn't really a success. What's happened to Hortense?'

'I'm looking after her.'

'You'd better watch out. She bites.'

93

'I know,' I said with feeling. 'What do you mean – it wasn't really a success?'

He was a man who took his time. He looked down at his hands for a moment, then said slowly: 'We were mates at university in England. Well, a bit more than mates really. I really liked Connie. She was a – a good person. I know that sounds incredibly naff, but I really mean it. She was sincere. Always ready to do someone a good turn. But shy. No, it was more than shyness. She was afraid to take risks. I wanted her to move in with me, but she wouldn't do it. She wouldn't take the plunge.'

'Did she have lots of friends?'

'No. Neither did I. It was one of those left-wing universities – everybody except us was really political. We didn't fit in all that well. That's probably partly why we got together. After our finals, Connie didn't know what she was going to do. I'd got this postgrad place out in Oz and I wanted her to come too, but she wouldn't.'

'So you went on your own?'

'Yes,' he said. He smiled. 'It was great. I loved it the minute I stepped off the plane. It was so different. I felt like a new person. I was able to do things I'd never had the nerve to do at home. I made friends, learned to ride, surfed, bummed around looking at the country – it was just great. After I'd finished my course I applied to stay on. I worked at all kinds of things – spent some time on a turkey farm, then worked in a garage in the city, then got my present job. Connie kept in touch all that time – she's a great letter-writer.'

'And you came back in 1985?'

'Yeah,' he said, thinking. 'She was already living here then. She seemed to be having a fine old time. She was different too – more lively, more fun. I really thought we'd got it together then. It was a great summer. Then I asked her to marry me. I wanted her to come on out to Oz with me.'

'And she wouldn't go?' I said.

He shook his head sadly.

'She wanted me to stay here with her. She had a good

job and all these friends and activities – she didn't want to have to start all over again in a strange place. But I didn't think I could live here, not after Australia. So at the end of the summer we called it a day and I went back. It was a bad scene at the time, but it was probably all for the best.'

'What made you decide to come and see her this time?'

'I wanted to see all my old friends,' he said, with that slow smile. 'I'm getting married next week and I figured I wouldn't be able to come to Europe again for a while, so I thought I'd take the opportunity to bum round and see everybody while I could – a sort of extended stag party. I wrote to Connie and she said she'd be pleased to put me up. But she'd changed so much I hardly recognized her. Well, I suppose I've changed too. You can't expect things to stay the same after so long.'

'Changed how? Connie, I mean?'

'Well, all the activities and friends – they seemed to have disappeared. She's living on her own with a neurotic cat, she's got this lousy job she doesn't like and she doesn't seem to be going out much at all. But I guess the main thing is that she's got this other guy.'

'Which other guy?' I asked instantly.

He looked rather abashed for a moment. 'Well, this sounds crazy, but I don't really know. I mean, she kept dropping these broad hints, but she wouldn't say anything outright about it. I thought she might be making it up – you know, because of me being engaged. But one day I heard them on the phone. They had a hell of a ding-dong – Connie was in her room but I could hear it through the wall. And afterwards she was crying and crying. She wouldn't tell me why. Then a couple of days later he rang up again and they seemed to make it up, because she was all smiles afterwards. But she wouldn't say anything about it. I guess she wanted to keep it secret because maybe he was married or something.'

'Did you hear what his name was?'

He frowned again. 'Yes, I did. Jesus, what the hell was it? I'm sorry, I've got a lousy memory for names, and

I only sort of overheard it once. A normal English man's name. Two syllables.'

'Graham?' I asked, like a pistol-shot.

'Could well have been. Yes, I'm pretty sure that was it.' He stopped for a second and frowned. 'Listen, are the police involved in this at all?'

'Yes, they are, but I don't think they know about you.'

'Oh, good,' he said. 'Can we keep it that way, if you don't mind? I've got to get on that plane for Oz tomorrow or I'll miss my own wedding and my mother-in-law'll kill me. But would you do me a favour? Could you let me know if you get any news about Connie? I'd like to know she's OK.'

We exchanged addresses and phone numbers, and then he shook my hand, shouldered his backpack and pushed off through the crowds. At the passport barrier he turned to wave. Connie must have been utterly bonkers, turning that down. In my hand was an address in Dundas, New South Wales, and a phone number.

I didn't wait to see his plane off. I had to do all my shopping and chores and get myself to the church on time. Six to be exact. Remembering the snooty looks I'd picked up at the art gallery, I took the trouble to put on a rather nice little linen dress I'd bought last time I was in Paris and a pair of green ear-rings that Giulia had given me for my birthday. Even I was pleased with the result. The first person I saw when I walked into the church was Isabelle Lefèvre, and the look she gave me was positively poisoned.

'Oh, it's you again,' she said.

'Me again,' I agreed cheerfully.

'And looking perfectly gorgeous, if I may say so,' Graham Ferguson said, close behind me. I turned. He was looking me up and down with an air of concentrated expectancy. He didn't exactly lick his lips, but the effect was the same.

'Matilda!' Vibeke came bustling over, pushing her husband out of the way. 'What a pretty dress! Hello, Isabelle. It's programme-selling this time. A hundred francs each.

Here's a float for both of you and the programmes are on the table over there.'

Programme-selling is all a matter of confidence and a big smile. People will buy anything if you smile at them. I went for it, got rid of all of my programmes in about fifteen minutes and had to go back for more. I even received a couple of tips. The Eglise des Minimes is a big church in the popular part of town known as the Marolles. Today it contained lots of hard-backed, hard-seated chairs arranged around a dais on which stood, yes, you've guessed it, a harpsichord and a number of music stands. There were crowds of people coming in.

'Programme, sir?' I asked, and stopped dead, because Aaron was standing in front of me, grinning like an idiot.

'I didn't know you liked this kind of stuff,' I said, taken aback, but not displeased.

'Neither did I. But I saw the poster you put up in the office. Meet me afterwards for a drink? How much are the programmes?'

He gave me a hundred-franc note and a twenty-franc tip. I was doing OK. That retirement villa on Lake Lugano was getting nearer by the minute.

A scattering of applause told me that something was happening on stage. The players were picking their way to their places, dressed in decent sober black, thank goodness. Julian Wychell appeared by my side.

'We've saved you a chair,' he said. 'Over by the pillar. They're just about to start.'

I'm not really into krummhorns, sackbuts and racketts. I supposed they played OK, judging by the applause at the interval, but I wasn't impressed.

'You don't like it,' Julian Wychell said.

'How can you tell?'

'You're scowling.'

'It's just not my favourite kind of music,' I said. 'Give me *The Ring* any day.'

'That's heavy-weight stuff,' he said with a laugh. 'My respect for you is increasing by the minute.' Then he added: 'You've got green eyes. I hadn't noticed before.'

'Hazel,' I said. 'It's the ear-rings that make them look green. What kind of music do you like?'

'Jazz,' he replied, with a smile. 'But seriously, they do play very well. They built the harpsichord themselves, you know.'

It didn't surprise me in the least.

'Come and have a drink,' Wychell said, getting up.

'In a church?'

'Follow me, fair lady, and all will be revealed.'

He led the way through a small wooden door into a large room which looked like, and indeed was, a church hall. The organizers were relaxing at a couple of trestle-tables. Open bottles of wine stood about. Several large open boxes and a certain whiff of oregano spoke of take-away pizza. Julian Wychell led the way over to one of the tables and pulled up a chair for me next to Graham Ferguson, who looked sideways and said: 'Hello!' in a way that was intended to sound vibrant with meaning. I found myself sitting opposite Vibeke, Isabelle and Françoise Wychell. Vibeke was smiling welcomingly, Isabelle was looking petulant, and Françoise Wychell was staring at the wall behind me.

Wychell seated himself on my other side, gave me a plastic cup, and said: 'Sorry, but there aren't any glasses. Would you like white or red wine?' I took white, and he poured. I refused the pizza; it looked as if it could do with a couple of weeks' holiday in a hot climate.

'Having fun?' Ferguson asked me.

'Matilda doesn't like Renaissance music,' Julian said, before I could answer.

'Something we've got in common, then.' Ferguson smiled down at me. 'Reminds me of when Imogen was playing in the school band, though actually I don't think this lot are as good.'

'Graham!' Vibeke exclaimed. 'They're very good indeed!'

'I'll take your word for it,' he answered.

Françoise had said nothing, but she was studying me closely. Her slightly hooded eyes were a cold greyish-green.

'Are you enjoying the performance, Madame Wychell?' I asked politely. There was a slight pause, as if she were making up her mind whether or not to honour me with a reply. Then she leaned forward and ground out her cigarette stub on an empty pizza-carton. 'I do not care for such music,' she said. I think it was the first time she'd spoken directly to me since we were introduced. She had a harsh voice and a rather heavy accent.

'It may be an acquired taste,' I said. 'But it probably takes about a millenium to acquire it.'

She didn't deign to answer. Close up, she had the dry lined skin of the heavy smoker. As the very thought whizzed through my mind, she reached down for her crocodile handbag and took out a heavy silver cigarette case. She lit another cigarette and puffed out a lungful of smoke, at the same time putting the case down on the table. It caught my eye: a beautiful piece, with an old-fashioned engraved coat of arms on it. It looked very out of place among the plastic trash and bits of pallid pizza crust.

'May I?' I asked, and picked it up before she could object. I might have known. The engraving was the de Jonckheere coat of arms. On the flip side, the silver was all puckered and dented. 'How strange,' I said. 'How did it get so damaged?'

She gave me another of those cold sea-water looks. Then she said: 'In the war. The First World War. My grandfather was in the cavalry and he was hit by sniper fire. He took one bullet in the shoulder and the cigarette case took the other.'

'You must be very proud of it,' I said, handing it back.

She said nothing, but her expression became a degree less icy.

As the conversation became more general, I suddenly felt Graham Ferguson's leg nudge mine. Accident? I glanced at him. He was looking straight ahead, a slight, absent smile on his lips. I moved a fraction. His leg followed, the length of his thigh clamped to mine. Accident my eye! Graham Ferguson was playing footsie, with his own wife sitting across the table. Now what was I supposed to do? Go along? Or give him the elbow and risk alienating him totally?

I bet Sherlock Holmes never had this trouble.

The problem solved itself. A harassed minion came in looking for Vibeke, who promptly got up and went out to solve whatever problem had arisen. The encroaching leg moved hurriedly. A general reshuffle ensued, during which I took the opportunity to get up and start clearing the table. Vibeke came back, saw what I was doing, and came to help.

Looking for plastic bags in the cupboard under the sink, I glanced over my shoulder in time to see Françoise rise, gather up her belongings, and move with her long stride to the door. She left a cigarette smouldering in the ashtray on the table. As we watched, Julian Wychell picked it up and stubbed it out, a patient look on his face. Beside me, Vibeke said softly: 'Poor man. He has a lot to put up with.' Her tone of voice told me a lot more than her words.

I looked at her quickly, in surprise. 'You mean Julian?'

She coloured a little and laughed. 'Yes, well, Françoise isn't the easiest of people to live with. But then I suppose none of us is perfect. We'll just put all the rubbish in these, shall we?'

I'd obviously stumbled on a certain hidden depth of feeling, but the last thing I wanted to do was intrude.

Isabelle had lost no time in following Françoise out of the room, and the two men were deep in conversation. Hoping it sounded casual, I asked Vibeke: 'By the way, is there any news of Karin Andersen? Is she feeling better?'

'Oh, but haven't you heard?' Vibeke said, surprised. 'She's gone back to Lund. Resigned from her job, packed everything up and left. I suppose it's the best thing – her family's there to take care of her. There was nothing for her here, really.'

I thought people weren't supposed to leave the country when involved in police enquiries. I could only surmise that the police had decided she had nothing to do with it. I wasn't so sure they were right.

The second half of the concert was no improvement on the first. My joints were starting to complain by the end. As soon as the last krummhorn was packed up, I nipped out to find Aaron and tell him I wouldn't be long. Luckily, there wasn't much clearing up to do – we only had to fold up the chairs and stack them in a small room at the back of the church. A quick sweep up of the discarded programmes and sweetie-wrappers on the floor, and that was that. I went to get my jacket.

'Here you are at last,' said Graham Ferguson, pushing the cloakroom door shut behind us.

Chapter 12

Oh, balooba. I was dumb not to have foreseen this. Now what?

'I've got to go,' I said. There wasn't time to think up anything more original.

Ferguson smiled. 'What's the hurry? Everybody's out there polishing the floor.'

'Someone's waiting for me.' I tried to edge to one side, reaching for my jacket.

'Let them wait,' Ferguson said, and advanced on me.

'Don't be daft,' I protested. 'What about Vibeke?'

'What she doesn't know won't hurt her,' he said, and grabbed me.

I just about managed to get my mouth out of the way in time, but he was a tall and strong man, and I found myself clamped against him in such a way that I couldn't move my arms or legs. Nor could I yell at the top of my voice – I couldn't risk everybody coming dashing in. That'd put the kybosh on the enquiry right enough.

'Get off! Goddamn it, Graham, get off!' I said, whipping my head frantically to and fro to avoid his attempts to kiss me. If I could get a hand free I could pull his hair or poke him in the eye or something. A shoe fell off as I kicked. Dammit, I was going to have to raise my voice.

The cloakroom door burst open and a voice said: 'Matilda!'

A moment later, I abruptly left Graham Ferguson's arms as he was unceremoniously yanked backwards. There was a scuffle and a short sharp yell. Then Ferguson was on the floor, his hands to his nose. Standing over him, fists clenched, every inch the Action Man, was Aaron.

You don't mess with Israelis. They learn unarmed combat in their cradles. Ferguson got to his feet, gasping, and backed off, groping in his pocket for a handkerchief. His nose was bleeding.

'I told you to let go,' I said.

He shot me a look of mingled dislike and fear, mopping at his nose.

'You led me on, you bitch,' he said. 'She led me on,' he added to Aaron.

I disposed of that with a short sharp word, and looked round for my shoe.

'Get out of here,' Aaron said, and Ferguson, who didn't appear inclined to argue the point, shuffled out, still gasping.

'You all right, Mat?' said my hero, coming towards me anxiously.

Well, I could have said that he'd blown the enquiry, but it would have been churlish under the circumstances.

'I'm fine,' I said. 'Perfectly fine. Thanks for your help, Aaron. You saved me a bit of bother.'

'Who was that guy anyway?' He bent, picked up my errant shoe, and handed it to me.

'One of the organizers. He's been coming on to me all evening.'

'He needs to be taught a lesson,' Aaron said, frowning. 'Are you sure you're OK?'

'Quite sure. Let's just go. He's got a nice wife, and I don't want to upset her. I don't suppose he'll bother me again.'

'If he does, you just let me know,' Aaron said. 'I'll fix him. Let's go and get that drink.'

There was no sign of Ferguson when we came out. We said goodnight to the others and made our way through the warm night to the nearest café. It was still early, but we didn't stay long. I was too preoccupied to be good company. I was trying to work out where to go from there. Aaron didn't seem to mind. Just being with me seemed to be enough. When he dropped me off, he asked:

'Do you want to go for a picnic tomorrow? It should be nice, if the weather holds.'

I was a little surprised, but there was no reason to say no, so I didn't. Anyway, a change of scenery might help my thought-processes.

Sunday was yet another beautiful midsummer day and the air smelled of warm grass as we roared down the motorway, with the top down and the back seat packed with food and wine and various items of picnicking gear. But when we reached the picnic-place, a quiet, flower-scattered meadow on the banks of the Lesse, I began to have misgivings.

To start with, the previous evening's events seemed to have induced a rather proprietorial air in my escort, which I wasn't sure I liked. Or maybe it was just the company. We were the only singles present. The others were all married couples with kids ranging from new babies to noisy, adventurous twelve-year-olds. They all knew Aaron well and were as friendly as could be, but the party immediately broke up along gender lines, the men setting up parasols and chairs and organizing the camp, while the women busied themselves with the food. I found myself firmly on the female side of the divide, and since there were small babies present, the conversation was predictably and exclusively about paediatrics.

Babies bore me to death. I tried to join in but there's a limit to endeavour, and my interest flagged after half an hour. The river looked beautifully cool and there were tempting paths leading off into the woods, but it would have looked boorish to abandon the group. I looked round for Aaron. The men were standing on the river bank discussing fishing, to judge by their gestures. The little boys were running about yelling, while a bunch of little girls was holding a dolls' tea-party near us. My feminist friends would have had coronaries, but what can you expect? Kids copy their parents. I stayed put while the beautiful golden morning crept by, feeling as if I were doing time.

We ate. The women served the food round to men and children alike, and then everyone except the liveliest kids took to the shade for a siesta. Aaron lay beside me, a straw hat over his eyes, his usually restless body at ease. He was enjoying himself in these family surroundings. I hadn't ever seen him so relaxed. I, on the other hand, felt like a whole circusful of jumping fleas. He reached up and tried jokingly to make me lie down, and when I resisted, he pushed the hat up and smiled at me.

'What's up?' he said. 'Relax, Mat, you're too uptight. It's a beautiful day. Enjoy.'

'I want to go for a walk.'

'Later, when it's cool,' he said. He pulled the hat down again and clasped his brown hands on his chest. His arms were earth-coloured, lightly covered with dark hair. I sat and waited till his breathing told me he was snoozing. Then I quietly got up and headed for the river.

There was a good path along the bank and I set off like an Olympic walker, full of charged-up energy. But after a while, I eased up and began to feel better. The sound of water running is a great tranquillizer. Every now and then a canoe went downstream with a soft plashing of paddles, but there was no one on the path at all.

People are always accusing me of being a loner, as if that's some kind of disease, but that's not the truth of it. The thing is that I don't care about belonging to groups. Nobody really understands it, except Georges, who's the same. It was a pity, I thought, that Connie wasn't here instead of me. She'd have loved it, this cosy family togetherness, but she'd chosen the path into the wilderness instead. I frowned. Where on earth had Connie got to? People don't just disappear, not in Belgium anyway. This isn't South America, after all.

As I retraced my steps, I thought of the interminable afternoon stretching before me, and felt the same dismal horror I used to feel at kids' parties when I was little. Come along now, Matilda. Don't sulk. You'll enjoy yourself if you make an effort and join in.

A few moments later, I met Aaron coming rapidly

in the opposite direction. He stopped when he saw me, looking relieved.

'Where did you get to? I was worried,' he said, and I had to laugh.

'I've got my compass and my Swiss Army penknife,' I told him. 'I'm ready for anything.'

'I thought you might have got lost.'

'I just needed some exercise,' I said. He took my hand and held it, which is something I particularly dislike, but I didn't want to seem impolite, so I left it there.

'We're going to organize some games,' he said. 'Come and join in.'

I hate games.

We all set off back to Brussels early, because of the kids. Aaron and I didn't talk much in the car. I couldn't think of anything but Connie, but Aaron didn't seem to mind my lack of conversation. He was in high spirits, humming snatches of song to himself, breaking off occasionally to smile at me. He was a really nice man. I felt as guilty as hell for not having enjoyed myself.

I couldn't settle down that evening. I walked round and round the flat, while Hortense, curled up in an armchair, shot me exasperated looks through half-closed golden eyes. What was I going to do now? There hadn't been any mention of Cultura's next activity, but I'd just have to hang in and hope for an opportunity to smooth down Ferguson's ruffled feathers. That was going to be a difficult job, and a long one too.

Chapter 13

I was awake most of the night and went to work tired. To my uneasy surprise, I found flowers on my desk. Nothing ostentatious, just a little bunch of white roses. I stopped short, staring, and slowly became conscious that everyone was looking at me. It was an open-plan office; you couldn't hide anything. There was a nasty hollow hush as I sat down and started sorting out my day's work.

A moment later, Aaron appeared and came straight over to me with a big smile. 'Mat, I've been thinking,' he said, hitching himself on to one corner of the desk. 'We've got so much work coming in, I could really do with an assistant. I've talked it over with Piet and Sam, and we figured you might fit the bill. The job's yours if you want it.'

There was nothing confidential about the communication; everyone had heard it. The office reverberated with silence. No wonder the atmosphere had cooled. They all thought I'd earned the job on my back. That interpretation obviously hadn't occurred to Aaron; his face was beaming with innocent pleasure at doing me a good turn.

I couldn't think what to say. Aaron saved me the trouble. 'Think it over and let me know,' he said. 'By the way, I thought you might like to come to the client presentation with me today. What about it?'

He might just as well have given me a sword and invited me to commit hara-kiri. I knew very well that he was supposed to be taking Bernie, our sharp little Kerry import; I could see her shocked face peering over one of the office partitions. Do something, Matilda.

'Well, thanks for suggesting it,' I said, finding my voice. 'But I've really got a lot of things to finish here. Another time, maybe.'

To my relief, he didn't insist. It was a bad morning. Shoulders were being worn very cold indeed. I sat, staring dismally into space. How could things change so quickly? Last week I was really having fun. I had, at last, an interesting and challenging job and a promising friendship with an attractive man. Now Aaron had moved in too fast and spoilt it all. How could a man of his experience be so naive?

Then, glumly, I remembered the girl who'd jilted him because he might 'cramp her career'. I remembered him saying how much he'd longed for normal family life as a kibbutz child; I remembered his obvious delight at being surrounded by kids and domestic paraphernalia at the picnic. A family man. Or rather, a man desperate for a family. I should have known. I should have seen the signs. Now it had gone so far that I only had one choice: cool the whole thing down and walk away. Damn, damn, damn.

I don't think I did much work that day. Georges called in the afternoon and we made a date to meet on Saturday evening to compare notes on the investigation. That was the sum of my day's efforts. I was glad to get home that evening.

Linda phoned; she'd had her baby and was home from the hospital. I hadn't got much to tell her, so she told me all about the birth, which I'd have much preferred her not to. I tried to make all the right noises. She'd heard nothing more from the police. I put the matter out of my mind and had a long conversation with Hortense. Hortense was beginning to like me; she hadn't bitten me for several days. Oddly enough, I was beginning to like her too.

First thing on Tuesday, I rang the agency and asked them to find me another assignment for next week. I told them there was a personality clash in the office. It was a pity. No, it was a crying shame, but I suppose that's the way it goes. Then I told Aaron that I couldn't take his job. I told him that it looked like favouritism and that the others resented it. He was shocked, then angry, not with me, but with the others. It was his company, and he'd damn well do as he liked. He'd have gone and bawled them all out if I hadn't told him that I'd be leaving on Friday and would prefer to let things ride for a while between us. He didn't like it at all. He spent the next three days trying to argue me out of it. Between that and the attitude of my colleagues, who were feeling guilty and remorseful now that I was leaving, it wasn't a happy week.

By Friday, I was glad to get out of there. The agency still hadn't found me anything for the next week, but I left just the same. I tried to slip out unobtrusively, but Aaron made a final attempt to get me to change my mind. He was upset and I was upset, and I only got home by dint of agreeing to see him again some time in the future. I was running late. I had a dinner date with Tonio and Giulia that evening.

I set off in a tired and rather frazzled mood. I have to say, however, that I was looking OK. Knowing that Giulia always wears black in the evening, I put on a lot of glitter and a little scarlet dress which looks like a Valentino, but isn't; when dining in Rome, dress like the Romans. I don't drive to dinner parties. My taxi was waiting downstairs and I was already heading for the door when the phone rang. Aaron, I thought, and my heart sank. I hesitated. Then it occurred to me that it might be Georges. I dashed over and grabbed the receiver. A voice said: 'Luc Vanderauwera.'

I nearly dropped the telephone. It had been weeks since our last encounter. What on earth did he want?

'I need to talk to you. Something very important. Are you in tonight?'

'No, I'm just on my way out. What is it?'

'I can't tell you on the phone,' he said. 'Where are you going? Can I meet you there?'

My mind started to gallop.

'I'm going to a dinner party —' I began, but he interrupted me.

'Where? I'll pick you up afterwards.'

It wasn't exactly what I wanted, but I couldn't think of an alternative quickly enough. I gave him the address.

'OK,' he said. 'What time?'

'Midnight?' I hazarded.

'OK,' he said again, and rang off. He hadn't become any more polite.

The taxi-driver was a round, cheerful little man who said that if he hadn't already got a wife and six children, he'd ask me to marry him. Was I going to the opera? He adored opera. He'd been a stage-hand at La Scala before coming to Belgium. He then sang me an aria from *La Bohème*, which was rather unseasonal as it was really very hot and my tiny hands were far from freezing. However, I was feeling much happier by the time I got to Tonio and Giulia's.

And bless their hearts, they'd hauled in a charming young Italian diplomat to flirt with me, and I could hardly disappoint them. What with the litres of Pinot Grigio going down, the evening was a decidedly relaxing one. Tonio and Giulia's friends are all rich, fashionable and quite without mercy, and the conversation scintillates with malicious charm. You have to get used to the fact that most of the women round the table have slept with Tonio and most of the men with Giulia.

It was a long and boozy meal. After the exquisite dessert, we retired in more or less good order to the drawing room. I'd say 'living room', but you can't imagine anyone living in that room; it looks like an opera set. We were settling down for coffee and *pousse-cafés*, when the little dark maid came in and whispered in Giulia's ear. Giulia looked startled, got up and quickly went out. I suddenly remembered that I had an assignation with the forces of law and order and looked at my watch. It was just before twelve. Three minutes later, Giulia was back, with a glitter in her eyes and a rather wicked smile. She held a hand up to still the conversation and announced: 'It's a policeman. He wants to see Matilda.'

For good effect, she repeated it in Italian and there was an interested buzz from the assembled company. My

Roman diplomat made a grab for my hand and missed, because I was already on my feet.

Out in the beautiful gleaming polished hall, Giulia took my arm and whispered: 'He's in the small salon. Take care, Matilda. He's very attractive, but he looks violent.' She shivered and gave a little laugh. I pulled away from her rather more abruptly than necessary and marched in. I could just imagine what Giulia would be telling the rest of her guests.

Vanderauwera had his back to the door and was staring at a sexy marble nymph on a stand. His general attitude conveyed glumness. As the door closed he turned round. There was a pause. He looked me up and down in a brief and amazed flash, and I remembered that on previous occasions, I had been dressed respectively for cleaning windows, mending cars and trawling gay bars. I waited. He cleared his throat.

'I'm sorry to interrupt your party,' he said rather awkwardly. He hadn't had much practice at apologizing. His gaze flickered down to my extremely low neckline again and then returned doggedly to my face.

'Can we go somewhere?' he asked. 'We can't talk here.'

The door opened wide and Tonio appeared, splendidly drunk. He looked at Vanderauwera with deep suspicion.

'Is this person bothering you, Matilda?' he said loudly, enunciating with care. 'Because if he is, I shall have him thrown out. No, just for you, I shall throw him out myself.'

I thought for a moment. 'He's a policeman,' I pointed out gently.

'He may be a policeman,' Tonio said with magnificence, 'but I – I am a diplomat.' He made another sweeping gesture, but had to let go of the door to do it, and nearly fell over.

Vauderauwera's face was stony, with a shade of contempt in it.

I said: 'I don't think it'll be necessary, Tonio. I was thinking of leaving, anyway. Would you make my excuses to Giulia?'

'She said to call her next week,' Tonio said, becoming

human again now he was sure that the ultimate sacrifice wouldn't be required. 'I shall tell her you have gone.'

With weaving steps, he made his way to an art nouveau *chaise-longue*, lay down carefully upon it and fell asleep. There was a silence.

Vanderauwera walked to the door and stood holding it for me. He waited in the hall while I went back to the party to make my excuses, but Giulia had disappeared with my diplomat and the others were all engaged in a vehement political discussion in Italian. Nobody was much interested to hear I was leaving. The little maid appeared with my jacket and helped me on with it. A moment later we were outside in the beautifully tailored garden. Vanderauwera breathed a sigh of relief, but made no comment about my friends, which was just as well, because I wasn't in the mood for more criticism. His car was waiting in the diplomatic parking space. Inside, there was a muted hum of static from the radio, broken by the occasional faint crackle of voices from somewhere in the night.

Vanderauwera reached forward abruptly and switched off the radio, then sat for a moment staring out through the windscreen in silence. Then he said: 'I've been told to drop the Connie Trevor case.'

Chapter 14

'What?' I said, incredulous.

He leaned forward and started the car.

'We'll go to a place I know,' he said.

It was a five-minute drive and we didn't talk, although my mind was ringing like an overworked cash-till. In a small dark dive of a café off the Place Flagey, he looked at me directly and repeated: 'I was told to drop the case this afternoon.'

'Why? By whom?'

He shrugged. 'It could be the Ministry of Justice, or the *Procureur du Roi*. Your guess is as good as mine. I was called by my father-in-law. He's chief of the brigade. He said we'd got more important things to do. I think he'd been leaned on by somebody higher up.'

The *patron* of the café came over and took our order. I had a fizzy water. I wanted a clear head. Vanderauwera asked for a Stella. The *patron* looked at the scarlet dress and all the glitter and not a flicker crossed his face. It probably happened every day.

'What's been going on?' I asked.

'I went to interview Graham Ferguson. I didn't like him. He was just too damned superior and sure of himself. Then I started making enquiries about him and this happened.'

'So that's why Karin Andersen was able to get out of the country,' I said.

'I've never seen anyone get on a plane so fast,' Vanderauwera said grimly.

'But surely they can't just decide the case is closed?'

The drinks arrived and I took a long pull at mine.

'They have,' Vanderauwera said.

'And if you don't toe the line?'

He put his empty glass down and shrugged again. 'Hassle. Suspension. My father-in-law's just dying for an excuse. I'm in trouble already.'

'What for?'

'Acting too much on my own initiative,' he said, adding rather derisively: 'You should understand that.' He turned towards the bar and signalled to the *patron* to bring another beer. Then turning back, he noticed my glass and said: 'Sorry, did you want another one?'

'No thanks. Why are you telling me? I thought we were sworn enemies.'

Another glass of Stella appeared at his elbow. He stared at me without saying anything for a moment, then said: 'No, not that.'

'Well, that's not how it feels at this end,' I said.

He put both hands on the table and looked down at them. I noticed he wasn't wearing a wedding ring.

He said: 'I know I come on too strong, too heavy. That's the job. You get like that. I resented an amateur getting in my way.'

'Hence the whistle-stop tour of the sewers?'

'I shouldn't have done that. If it makes any difference, I felt like a bastard afterwards.'

'Good,' I said uncompromisingly.

He looked at me for a long moment.

'You really are a tough one,' he said.

'Coming from you, that has to be a compliment,' I answered, and suddenly, despite himself, he smiled. It turned him into a human being instead of a Flemish version of Robocop, and I would have had to have been dead not to have smiled back. Giulia's right, I thought, he is attractive.

It's amazing what a couple of smiles can do. I almost heard the thin crackle of ice melting.

'Well, what are you going to do?' I asked.

'Carry on with the enquiry.' He raised his eyebrows as if it were a stupid question.

114

'And your career?'

He drained the glass of beer and put it down on the table with a sharp sound.

'That's my business,' he said. He turned again and gestured to the *patron*.

The movement pulled his jacket back and I caught a glimpse of a shoulder-holster underneath. I know the Belgian police carry guns as a matter of course, but I'd never sat at a table with an armed man before. He saw the expression on my face and the direction of my stare, and gave me a derisive look.

'We need the protection,' he said, bitterly ironical.

'What kind of gun is it?' I asked, curious.

'Nine millimetre Browning. Standard *Gendarmerie* issue. Do you know anything about guns?'

'No. They didn't cover that at secretarial college.'

'You surprise me,' he said.

There was a silence. The background tape was playing a Jacques Brel song, a poem to the beauty of Flanders, with its wide skies and mirror-surfaced canals, its misty plain punctuated by cathedrals, its deserted dunes and the cold North Sea licking at its shores. We listened without speaking. At the end, Vanderauwera said, unexpectedly:

'He wrote a song for you too. Did you know?'

' "Mathilde",' I replied. 'I know it. It's not a very flattering comparison.'

'Oh, I don't know,' he replied. His gaze wandered down to my bare shoulders again, almost involuntarily.

The Stellas were beginning to relax him. I frowned and got back to the point.

'OK, so you're going to carry on,' I said, leaning back. 'Why drag me out of a dinner party to tell me?'

'Because I need your help. They've tied my hands. They've closed the Connie Trevor case and dumped half a dozen other cases on me. That means I'll have less time and fewer resources. So I need you to do it for me.'

He really had nerve. I stared, uncertain whether to laugh at the sheer cheek of it, or to be very, very angry.

'Why on earth are you bothering?' I asked finally. 'You didn't seem particularly interested in the case before.'

'Nobody orders me off a case,' he said, and I heard his teeth grind. 'And I don't like Mr Graham Ferguson. If he's behind this, which I think he must be, then he's got something to hide, and I'm going to find out what it is.'

'Even if you get kicked out of the force?'

'Yes,' he said. His jaw was clamped so tight that I could see the joint of the bones through the skin.

I could have said: 'Why the hell should I do anything for you, buster?' I could have said: 'Go take a long running jump in a very cold lake.' I could have said: 'I'd rather be knee-capped, thanks.'

Instead I said: 'OK.'

The tape was now playing '*Je t'aime, moi non plus*' and for some reason, Jane Birkin's heavy breathing seemed to get to Vanderauwera, for he looked up and winced. Wondering if I needed a brain-scan, I said: 'Remember I told you I had a friend in the Ministry of the Interior?'

'Everybody's got a friend in the Ministry of the Interior,' he replied wearily.

'Do you want to know this or don't you? This guy moves in the same circles as the Fergusons and he's promised to make some enquiries. I'm meeting him tomorrow at eight to see what he's got. Do you want to come?'

He looked sharply at me. 'You told your friend all this? How the hell do you know it wasn't him who leaned on the police?'

'Because I've known Georges for years and I trust him. He helped me get at Ferguson, for heaven's sake. Come and see for yourself.'

'You got at Ferguson?' he interrupted. 'When?'

'Over the last couple of weeks. And I don't believe he's telling the truth about Connie either. For one thing, she was apparently his secretary. Did he tell you that?'

'*God verdomme!*' Vanderauwera exclaimed, not quite under his breath. 'No wonder he was on the defensive when I spoke to him. He'd already had the Haycastle treatment. What did you do, hang him from the ceiling by his ankles?'

'Don't be daft. He doesn't know anything about me.

116

I've just been hovering round hoping to pick up information.'

'And have you?'

'Not a lot yet. I can't just go up and ask him. But Karin Andersen turned up the other night and spilled the beans about Connie, and Ferguson really looked rattled. He hadn't told anyone about the police enquiry, not even his business partner.'

My ear-rings were pinching. Absent-mindedly I pulled them off and put them on the table, where they lay like little glittering snakes.

'I talked to an ex-boyfriend of Connie's from Australia. He'd been staying with her just before she went on holiday. He said he heard her calling her new boyfriend and he was sure the guy's name was Graham. He says they had a nasty quarrel over the phone and then apparently made it up a couple of days later.'

There was a silence. Vanderauwera picked up one of my ear-rings and held it in his palm, studying it.

'What do you think of Ferguson?' he asked, not looking up.

'He's a superior creep with a northern chip on his shoulder. And he's all hands. Not the kind of man I'd like to get stuck in a lift with. Will you come tomorrow? I know it's short notice for a Saturday night. You've probably already got something else lined up.'

'No,' he said. 'I'll come. We've found the man from the train, by the way. He's a student called Terry Evans and he lives with his parents in Buckinghamshire somewhere.'

'Did you talk to him?' I asked eagerly.

'No. The English police interviewed him and sent us a copy of the statement. He had his pocket picked in Florence and Connie lent him a couple of thousand francs to see him on to his boat back to England. All totally innocent.'

'He didn't know where she was going?'

'No. He saw her go towards the métro and that's all. He just changed platforms and caught the train for Ostend.'

'What about Ann Wilcox and the famous Nigel?'

117

'Not a thing,' he said. 'They've apparently disappeared into thin air. The English police can't find them. Even the family in Swindon doesn't know where they are. But at least they told us Nigel's other name: it's Grant.'

'And Karin Andersen?'

'A basket-case,' he said. 'She hated Connie all right, but there's no real proof to link her in.'

'Except that she knows the Fergusons,' I reminded him.

'That's not a crime,' he said. 'And anyway, she's gone now.'

There was another silence. Then I said, rather hesitantly, for I had my own fears and was reluctant to have them confirmed: 'What do you think has happened to Connie?'

'I don't know,' he replied. 'But I'm beginning to think it may be something very unpleasant.'

He dropped me off at my apartment, saying he would pick me up the following evening. It was very late. I wondered briefly what his wife thought about the hours he kept, and then reflected that she must be used to it, especially if she was a policeman's daughter as well as a policeman's wife. That thought brought back unpleasant memories and I shivered. I suddenly felt very tired. A holiday would be great. I could drive down to Arles and spend a couple of weeks soaking up the sun and exploring the Camargue. I sighed and stared rather bleakly at myself in the mirror. My hair was coming down and my mascara had smudged, which gave me a decadent look, especially in that dress. Was that why Vanderauwera had been reminded of Brel's beautiful, restless Mathilde, who has her hapless young man tied up in knots?

Go to bed, Matilda.

Chapter 15

Saturdays are always a mad rush for working women. The day Europe switches to Sunday shopping, I personally shall stand up and cheer. But we're still in the dark ages, so, as usual, I spent my Saturday dashing from supermarket to launderette to do-it-yourself centre and got back to my apartment exhausted in the early evening. I'd barely had time to change and sit down for a chat and a game with Hortense when the doorbell rang and Vanderauwera came up. He was wearing jeans and a leather jacket and looked even more like a thug than usual. I made coffee and came back into the living room to find that Hortense was lying on her back in his lap, having her tummy tickled.

'That cat's a fifth columnist,' I said.

I got the second smile then. If he wasn't careful, it might become a habit.

I'd warned Georges that I was bringing a possibly hostile stranger and Georges had reacted in typical fashion by putting out another bottle of wine. He greeted Vanderauwera with his usual urbanity, and Vanderauwera stared at him with barely concealed suspicion. There was a rather awkward pause. Looking from one to the other, I said: 'The Inspector thinks you may have shopped him, Georges,' and got a glare from the Inspector which would have withered me in my size sixes had I been made of less stern stuff.

'Indeed?' Georges said, raising his eyebrows as high as they could possibly go. 'A plausible theory, but not, alas, a correct one. But of course, you only have my word for that. Please sit down, both of you, and have a glass of wine. I gather that you have been requested to drop the case, Inspector? That seems most suspicious to me, knowing, as I do, only too well the nefarious habits of our countrymen.'

Vanderauwera was looking rather dazed, as well he might, though whether it was a result of the Chassagne-Montrachet or Georges's inimitable style of English, I couldn't tell.

'Anyway,' Georges pursued, with a rather malicious smile, 'in for a penny, in for a pound, as they say. What have you discovered, my beautiful Matilda?'

I ran through it all again, for Georges's benefit. I was beginning to think I could do it to music.

'Interesting,' Georges said, when I finished. 'It all ties in rather well with what I have discovered.'

Georges's manservant Albert came in with an assortment of bits and pieces on a platter and put them down on the table. Georges wandered over to the window and stood there for a moment looking at us.

'As you probably already know, Ferguson is a lawyer by profession, born and educated in the north of England.'

'But not at a public school,' I said.

'Is that important?' Vanderauwera enquired, raising his brows.

'He thinks so,' I said. 'So it probably is.'

'A good grammar school,' Georges continued. 'Followed by a respected Yorkshire university. He is a clever man, but his later career has not lived up to his early brilliance. He gained a first-class degree, spent some years in London and then moved to Sweden, where he met and married his wife.'

'Who is perfectly charming,' I said.

'Indeed she is,' Georges agreed. 'They moved to Brussels some five years ago, and he found a job on a Commission project to do with computing standards.'

'PICTS?' I asked sharply.

'PICTS,' he agreed.

'So Connie *was* his secretary?'

'She worked for him for about three months. Then her

contract ran out and was not renewed. The interesting thing is that Ferguson was not popular at the Commission. Very few people have a good word to say for him. He is, according to report, a clever bastard. He also appears to be a man who changes his job frequently. Every two or three years, as a rule.'

'Companies close down,' I said. 'People are forced to change.'

Georges shook his head gently.

'Not in this case. All the changes were voluntary. He never seems to have trouble finding a new job, mostly very highly paid.'

'Clever lawyers never do,' Vanderauwera put in.

'Ferguson left PICTS two years ago and joined De Jonckheere and Wychell. The Fergusons and Wychells have known one another for a number of years. There is nothing on his record except for the usual number of parking and speeding fines. His wife is from a diplomatic background and is an extremely popular figure in the Swedish expatriate community. He has two daughters, Imogen and Mona, both at the Scandinavian School. There is no shortage of money – he is apparently a shrewd investor.'

'Affairs?' Vanderauwera asked.

'No definite information. However, he is generally reputed to be a ladies' man.'

'I wouldn't call it that,' I said with feeling. 'He's a four-handed grabber.'

Georges looked at me with amusement. 'Do you speak from personal experience, my Matilda?'

'He jumped on me in the cloakroom. What's more, he's had a lot of practice. And I'd say he'd have no scruples at all about cheating on his wife. His attitude is that what she doesn't know won't hurt her.'

'Did you extricate yourself with decorum?' Georges enquired, looking mildly concerned.

'Not exactly,' I said. 'A friend of mine dashed in and poked him in the nose.'

There was a short silence. Vanderauwera stared at me

with a frown. Then Georges said, with commendable understatement: 'Will that not make further enquiry difficult?'

'Yes, it will. But what choice have we got? I'll have to do the best I can. But I can't understand what in the world Connie saw in him. I wouldn't have thought he was her type at all.'

'There is no accounting for tastes. Ferguson is wealthy and not bad-looking, and history is full of good women who have thrown their caps over the windmill for bounders. So you will continue your enquiries?'

I nodded.

'And you, Inspector?'

'The same.'

'Forgive me,' Georges said. 'But why should you wish to continue with this case? To spite your father-in-law?'

The temperature dropped about sixty degrees and, for a moment, the dangerous look was back on Vanderauwera's face. Then he said: 'Call it professional pride. I don't like unfinished cases.'

'I see,' Georges said. 'Well, finish up the wine. I'm afraid I shall have to throw you both out now, much as it pains me. I have an appointment for a late supper.'

I stared in amazement. This abrupt dismissal was totally unlike Georges. Usually he was lavishly hospitable. I'd been expecting food and consequently hadn't had anything to eat before coming out.

Vanderauwera asked if he could make a call and was escorted to the telephone room by Albert. It always kills me that Georges gives the phone a room to itself. As the door closed, Georges shot me a glance that I can only describe as sly and said: 'That young man has a dangerous face. You know what he makes me think of? A crusading knight, off to Jerusalem to seek the Holy Grail.'

Taken by surprise, I gave a snort of laughter. 'Come on, Georges, you've been listening to too much Wagner.'

But Georges shook his head.

'Oh, yes indeed. The mouth gives it away: pent-up passion. You should be careful, Matilda. I suspect his motives in wishing to continue with this investigation. I doubt if he would be so assiduous if you were fat and ugly with a moustache.'

I made a derisive noise. 'You're as bad as Giulia. I think you're both crackers. Firstly, he's a policeman. Secondly, he's married, and thirdly, I don't leap into bed with every man I meet and not every man I meet wants to leap into bed with me.'

Georges's eyebrows disappeared over the top of his head. 'Be careful,' he repeated. 'I would say that rape might be just up his street.'

'Nobody rapes Vandals,' I said.

'He looks as if he might like to try,' said Georges.

Georges likes to have the last word.

Outside in the street, Vanderauwera said, somewhat to my surprise: 'Let's get something to eat.'

I had no objection. We went to a Portuguese place which was noisy and cheerful and welcoming. It was also crowded, but the people in the restaurant knew Vanderauwera and they quickly cleared a small table, whisked down paper tablecloth, napkins and utensils and seated us with smiles and cheerful faces. Deciphering the menu took up all our attention for the first five minutes, by which time the wine had arrived.

For some reason, possibly to do with Georges's Burgundy, I was feeling light-hearted; I can't remember what I talked about to begin with, but I must have been doing well, because Vanderauwera smiled a couple more times during the first course. However, we'd barely started on our main dish before the tired frown suddenly reappeared on his face. A moment later, a high-pitched woman's voice said behind me: '*Tiens! Luc! Quelle surprise!*' and our tiny table was surrounded by a crowd of fashionable-looking people who exclaimed shrilly at seeing him, commented on how tired he was looking, glanced curiously at me, asked rather pointedly after his wife, made effusive, hand-shaking goodbyes and then mercifully left, rudely leaving the restaurant door open behind them.

'Friends of yours?' I asked, in the ensuing silence.

'No, not mine. Marie-Paule's. My wife.'

She had a name now. Marie-Paule. His wife. Suddenly I felt that there were three of us sitting at the table.

'And they're going to tell her you were seen hobnobbing with an unknown female?' I said, trying to sound light.

'I don't care if they do,' he answered, and there was so much bitterness in his voice that I decided to leave the matter there, and instead applied myself to my pork Alentejano. But a moment later, he looked up and said abruptly: 'I'm sorry. Let's talk about something else. Do you think you can get any more information hanging around with the Fergusons?'

'I can try,' I said. 'Has it occurred to you that even if we can prove Connie and Ferguson were lovers, it doesn't necessarily mean anything?'

'Yes,' he said. 'It has. But I don't like the sound of this quarrel she had on the phone. I'd like to talk to that chap in Australia, if you'll give me the number. And I want to find your Ann Wilcox. It's rather suspicious that she's disappeared off the face of the earth just at this particular moment. It smells wrong. I'm better placed than you to pursue that angle.'

'Sure, but don't let your father-in-law catch you. He'll have you transferred to Tubize.'

Tubize, at the risk of offending the Tubizians, is the pits.

'I don't care if he does,' Vanderauwera said again. 'I'm sick of being the poor idiot who gets pushed around. I'm going to do some pushing now.'

He began to eat with renewed energy. I stared at him, Georges's words in my mind. As it happened, the dim light in the restaurant threw the austere bones of his face into relief and Georges's remarks suddenly seemed rather apt after all. The thought brought with it a disturbing, but definite flicker of lust. To cover it, I said: 'Do you still think Georges is a mole?'

'No. Just crazy, like all your friends.'

'Thanks for the compliment,' I said, a little ruffled.

He looked up, and for a long moment, we stared

directly at one another. His face gave nothing away at all. I said: 'What are you staring at? Have I got gravy on my chin?'

He glanced away with a slight smile and said: 'No. A cat may look at a king.'

I relaxed and laughed. 'That's one of my mother's favourite sayings.'

'Your mother's French, isn't she? And your father's English? Where do they live?'

'Near Sevenoaks. That's in Kent, in the south.'

'I know it,' he said, and I remembered that he had English relatives too. 'How did they meet?'

'My father's a scientist – did a lot of valuable war work on radar and that kind of stuff. He met my mother at a scientific conference in Paris in 1955 – she was an interpreter. She's much younger than he is.'

'Does she like England?'

'Not much. He was doing research, and she had all these romantic ideas about living in beautiful old university towns and hobnobbing with professors and the cream of the English academic world. It all turned out rather differently. My father's always been completely absorbed in his work – never had much time for hobnobbing with anyone, or even for normal family life, come to that. My mother came down to earth with rather a bang.'

And since he seemed disposed to listen, I told him more about my mother, and the little corner of France she's built around herself in the English countryside. The French take unkindly to exile. In return, to my surprise, Vanderauwera talked about his own mother, widowed now, but unwilling to return to an England that had become a foreign country to her. There she still was, Maggie Watkins of Petts Wood, living in the pretty Flemish town of Lier and very happy. He liked Lier himself. He started telling me about it. He used to play football for a local team; he still went and kicked a ball around with his old friends when he went back.

All of a sudden, imperceptibly, the edgy antagonism between us had disappeared. We seemed to have stumbled by accident on to safe ground: the past impersonal. We talked about our childhoods, our schooldays, about Belgium and England, about everything except the present. I'd gathered, more from what he hadn't said than from what he had, that all was not well with his marriage, but it wasn't any of my business and I asked no questions. Similarly, he'd not trespassed on the subject of my current circumstances, though it did occur to me, somewhat uncomfortably, that maybe that was because he'd already investigated them. Nor did we talk about Connie.

I already knew he was intelligent and cynical and tough; as he relaxed, I discovered he could also be entertaining. He was stimulating company. We were finishing dessert and I was thinking with amazement that this was a man I could really get to like, when he glanced up behind me and the shutters slammed down again, just like that.

I turned in my chair and, to my horror, there stood Aaron, looking tight-lipped. The whole world was in that damned restaurant that evening. I have to admit that I was flustered. I said something bright and witless, and Aaron, barely glancing at Vanderauwera, said tightly:

'I went round to your flat this afternoon, but you weren't there.'

There's no answer to a remark like that.

'Matilda, we've got to talk,' he said. 'Can I come by and see you tomorrow? Please?'

There was nothing I could do except agree. We arranged to meet at three the following afternoon, at my flat. Aaron said goodnight and left. There was a short pause. Then Vanderauwera, all the ice back on, said: 'One of the boyfriends?' and, rattled, I snapped, 'It's none of your business!' and we were right back where we started. I didn't try and explain. Why should I? He drove me home in silence, and I could feel the pork and scallops quarrelling inside me already.

When he drew up outside my apartment, he said: 'Where are you working next week?'

'I haven't got anything at the moment. You can get me at home. How can I get in touch with you?'

'You can't,' he said, staring out through the windscreen. 'You'd better not call me at the office. Wait for me to call you. I can't say when that'll be; I've got a busy schedule next week.'

There's something very intimate about being in the front seat of a small car with a man. I was suddenly conscious that his hand on the gear-lever was only a few centimetres from my knee. But the atmosphere between us was raw and unsettled, all the more so in contrast to our previous ease. I searched for something to say and failed, so I just said: 'OK,' and got out and watched him drive away.

I couldn't sleep that night: maybe it was the scallops. I walked restlessly around the apartment for a while, wishing the evening hadn't ended on such a sour note. Hortense, taking advantage of my lowness of spirits, weaselled her way into the bedroom and settled down beside me, purring. I let her stay, and regretted it when she decided to get up and walk all over me at five in the morning.

I looked awful and felt worse by the time Aaron arrived, and was in no state to handle what turned out to be a thoroughly depressing interview. I was expecting the worst and I got it. He was in love with me. He couldn't sleep thinking about me. There had never been anything in his life like this before and he wanted to marry me and settle down and have kids with me. Please say yes, Matilda. Matilda, speak to me. Have I offended you in any way?

It's the most difficult thing in the world to tell a nice, kind, attractive, devoted man that you're very fond of him, but you don't love him. That his cosy dream of a close-knit and devoted family is your worst nightmare. That you don't want to be protected and looked after and sheltered from the world. He wouldn't believe it. He realized he was rushing me; he knew that three weeks was too short a time to make up my mind; he'd give me all the time I wanted, all the time I needed. How could I tell him that no amount of time would make any difference? I tried, as kindly as I could, but you can't make that sort of thing kind. He wanted to go on seeing me, but I said gently that there would be no point.

He fell silent for a moment, and then he mentioned Luc Vanderauwera. I said that Vanderauwera was a business contact, and Aaron didn't believe me. I wasn't prepared to argue it out, however. We said a few rather bitter, final things to one another and then Aaron left, and I sat down with a raging headache. It wasn't a good Sunday.

Chapter 16

On Monday morning I suddenly remembered that my blessed handbag had been at the *cordonnier*'s for weeks, ever since the break-in. At least I had the time to go and fetch it now. I drove round, hoping that the cobbler wasn't shut for his annual holiday, as most small businesses are in July. He was still open. He didn't take holidays, he told me, handing me the parcel. Couldn't afford to, what with the income tax and the VAT and the social security and this new ecological tax. This government was squeezing the people dry. There'd be a revolution one day, see if there wouldn't.

Back home, I transferred all my gear from the bag I'd been using, and opened the side pocket to put my keys in. There was a bundle of paper in the side pocket. What was that doing there? A bit of junk mail, and a letter. I tossed out the junk mail and tore the envelope open.

An English fifty-pound note fluttered out as I unfolded the sheet of paper.

'Dear Miss Trevor,' it said. 'I thought I should write straight away and thank you . . .'

What?

Then I remembered the letter I'd taken from Connie's mail-box the day of the burglary and shoved into my bag for future reference. I'd forgotten all about it in the subsequent excitement. I scrabbled for the envelope. An English stamp. The letter itself bore a printed return address.

Maplehurst,
10 Lacy Road
High Wycombe,
Bucks.

Dear Miss Trevor,
I thought I should write straight away and thank you for your kindness in helping me out last Sunday. Without your two thousand francs, I'd never have made it to the coast, let alone England. I enclose fifty pounds in repayment, with my grateful thanks. I hope you enjoyed the rest of your holiday.
Yours sincerely,
Terry Evans.

The telephone was in my hand before I'd even finished the letter.

It only took a few minutes to get through to the Evans household. Directory Enquiries found the number for me and a rather vague woman's voice answered almost at once. It was Mrs Evans. Yes, Terry was at home. She'd get him. I heard her voice calling, then the sound of someone bounding down the stairs and a couple of words exchanged between them. Then he came on. It was a school captain's voice, youthful but responsible. The police had already talked to him, he said, but he hadn't been able to tell them very much.

'Miss Trevor was awfully kind. I'd have been in real trouble if it hadn't been for her. It was my own fault, I suppose. I know I shouldn't have left my wallet in my back pocket. It's simply asking to have it stolen. Luckily, they didn't get my passport and ticket as well. Anyway, I didn't discover it till I was in the dining car. I wanted to pay for my supper and I didn't have any money. Miss Trevor was at the same table – they'd put us together because we were both travelling alone.'

'So she bailed you out?'

'She paid for my supper and then gave me extra to get home. It was really kind of her, because she didn't know me from Adam. Of course, I promised to repay her and I sent her the money as soon as I got home.'

'I know,' I said. 'What happened when you got to Brussels?'

'I carried her suitcase up to the station concourse, and then she helped me find out which platform the Ostend train was leaving from. That was all.'

'And where was she headed?'

'The underground.'

'Do you know where she was going?' I asked. 'Did she mention a place – the name of a station or anything?'

There was a silence. Then he said doubtfully: 'She mentioned a name that sounded like Tom Burr. But I don't know if that was a person or a station.'

I mentally reviewed the Brussels métro system in a single lightning flash. Luckily, the Brussels métro system is a relatively small one. Thank heavens it wasn't Paris.

'Could it have been Tomberg?' I asked, inspired.

'It might. Yes, it could well have been. And she said she was spending the rest of her holiday at a friend's flat.'

That was news to me. 'Did you tell the police that?' I asked.

There was a silence. Then he said: 'I think so.' But he didn't sound all that sure. He added: 'Honestly, that's all I can remember.'

'Did she mention if the friend was male or female?'

'No. I say, nothing's happened to her, has it?'

'That's what I'm trying to find out,' I said rather grimly. I thanked him for his help and rang off.

For some reason I couldn't stay in the apartment after that. It was a lovely afternoon, the height of summer. Brussels is wonderful in July. All the people with kids go on holiday, and most of the town is warm and beautiful and deserted. The parks are green and shady, the churches are empty, the streets are blessedly free of traffic. I took the tram out to the forest and went for a long walk. It's like being in a cathedral; the beech trees are tall and straight like pillars and far overhead you can hear the

131

wind in the green roof of leaves. I met one or two people walking dogs, and about a dozen squirrels. No one else. It was completely quiet, except for a woodpecker now and then, or a sudden screech from a jay. I might have been on another planet. You'd never have thought a major city was almost a stone's throw away. The soil smelled dry – we hadn't had rain for a while and the ground was thirsty. I walked for a couple of hours, my feet hardly making any print on the ground. If I disappeared off the face of the earth that very minute, no one would ever know what had happened to me. It was not a comforting thought.

After a while I crossed a road and found myself in the domesticated part of the forest: the Bois de la Cambre, which is parkland. I don't know who was responsible for landscaping the Brussels parks, but he or she was a genius. Every tree is chosen with care, every hill and dell curved to perfection. The Bois looks wonderful in every season. In July, it is a symphony of mature green. I think green is the most beautiful colour in the world. I walked round the lake, which is the centrepiece of the park, and sat down on a bench near the line of fountains at the end. A broad path runs round the lake; it's a favourite afternoon walk for the *Bruxellois*, particularly *après*-lunch: just long enough to make you feel you've had a breath of fresh air, but not too long to exhaust you.

I watched them go by: women with toddlers and laden prams; groups of students deep in noisy argument; middle-aged ladies in expensive silk afternoon dresses and high-heeled shoes; dogs and dog-owners of every description. Sweaty, fanatical-looking joggers in headbands pounded past, staring fixedly ahead. Young couples went by slowly, hand in hand. A pair sat down on the bench next to mine; after a quick glance at me to make sure I wasn't likely to make any stuffy objections, the young girl plonked herself down on the boy's knees and they went into a prolonged and passionate embrace. I thought that it was a long time since I'd been kissed in a public park. It was a damn long time since I'd been kissed properly at

132

all. Aaron's decorous embraces had hardly counted. I pushed the thought of Aaron out of my mind. I felt rotten about Aaron. I found myself, almost against my will, speculating about Luc Vanderauwera.

The pair next to me must have been breathing through their ears; they hadn't come up for air for at least three minutes. They looked about sixteen, but they probably weren't. Students look younger every year to me. I stared morosely across the water at the ferry crossing slowly to the little island in the middle of the lake. I envied these kids their opportunities. When I was sixteen, I was busy studying for exams. When I was eighteen, I was busy studying for exams. When I was twenty-one, I was busy studying for exams. I hit the market late as far as men were concerned. It's a bit like tackling the Grand National without ever having raced before. If you don't fall on your face, you learn a lot in a very short time.

The sun was going down slowly and the park was beginning to empty. The young couple disentwined themselves and wandered off, hand in hand. It was the best time of the evening. The sky was turning violet and it was still warm. But it was late and I'd been out for hours. When I got up, I realized that my feet were aching. I went slowly towards the edge of the park. Shadowy rabbits had come out and were nibbling at the grass. I took a tram into town and had a plate of noodles at my local Vietnamese café, then, reluctantly, went home. Hortense disapproved of my absence and showed it by refusing to eat her supper.

Nobody called that evening. I was in an oddly depressed mood. I really didn't want to go on thinking about Luc Vanderauwera because there was no point, but I couldn't help remembering, with a strange bereft feeling, the short time of friendship between us. Aaron had arrived just at the wrong time. Well, that was the way it went sometimes.

House-cleaning may be beneath the dignity of many modern women, but it's a hell of a good cure for the blues. I got up determined to clean the flat from top to bottom and by three o'clock in the afternoon, I had worked myself into cheerfulness again. I changed a couple of blown light bulbs, polished the silver, took my washing to the launderette, fixed the leak in the loo, and hung up three pictures that had been waiting since Christmas for me to get round to them. I went to the bank to pay a few bills, got my hair washed and trimmed, bought some new eye make-up and came home feeling a new woman. As I came in, the phone began to ring.

I shan't say I sprinted across the room, but I certainly moved with some speed.

It was Linda. She was incoherent with excitement, so much so that at first I couldn't work out what she was trying to say.

'Oh, Matilda, she's all right, she's all right! We've heard – we've had a letter. She's sent us a letter. She's all right!'

'What? Who? Linda! Who's sent you a letter?'

'Connie! It's Connie! It was all a false alarm. She's in America. I've got the letter here.'

'Connie?' I croaked, disbelieving, but Linda was unstoppable.

'Oh gosh, my fingers are trembling, I can hardly . . . She wrote it from the Flamingo Motel in Malibu. Listen to this! "Dear Linda, I know this will be a surprise to everyone, but I've decided to take the plunge and do what I've always wanted to – travel round the US. I'm in California at the moment. I managed to find a bit of work as a typist – in the black, of course! It seems to be quite easy. Next week I'm off to the Pacific North-West and then Wyoming and Montana. Doesn't that sound wonderful? I've got a special deal on American Airlines and anyway I've got plenty of money saved up, so don't worry about me. I'll be back in about six months' time, unless I decide to stay here, which I might do, because it's really marvellous. Everyone says English secretaries can find jobs easily over here. After all, I don't have any ties in Brussels. It's about time I had some fun, and if I don't start now, I never shall. I'll write and let you know how I get on. Love to you and all the family, Connie." There, what do you think of that?'

I hardly knew what to think. I recognized Connie's girlish, breathless style.

'Is that all she says?'

'Yes, it's just a short letter. I found it waiting when I got back from shopping this afternoon. I rang you straight away. Oh, Matilda, I'm so glad! Isn't it marvellous?'

'Are you sure it's from Connie? Is it her writing? Are you really sure?'

'Oh yes, absolutely. The letter itself is typed, but the signature's Connie's, and the envelope's handwritten. It's her writing all right. Oh, Matilda, everything's all right after all.'

My mind was whirling round like one of those windmills on sticks that kids play with. I think I said all the right things, how glad I was and yes it was wonderful etc., and asked after David and the new baby, but after I'd put the phone down, I sat and stared at it for a long time with a frown on my face. I spent the rest of the day mooning round the flat, unable to settle to anything.

What was wrong with me? Why wasn't I happy and delighted at the news, just like Linda?

Because I didn't believe it, that's why. Not after what Terry Evans had told me. Connie had left him to spend a week at a friend's flat, not to go to America. Would she have bothered to mislead a total stranger she'd just met on the train? For that matter, would any woman have come home from two weeks' holiday in Italy and gone straight to get on a plane for the US without going home to do her dirty washing and repack her suitcase?

And another reason was sitting by the kitchen door with her round golden eyes fixed speculatively on me and her black velvet ears pricked. I patted my knee invitingly, and Hortense leapt up with a small chirp of pleasure and settled down purring.

'It all comes back to you, doesn't it?' I said.

I stroked back the short fur along the sides of her fine little triangular head and she lifted her nose, her eyes closed in bliss. She looked like one of those carvings you see in the Egyptian department of the Louvre. Without

Hortense, the letter might just about have seemed credible. But there Hortense indubitably was, and I would bet my last centime that Connie would never, never have left her cat to starve to death. Not in a million years.

Chapter 17

Whatever would we nosey-parkers do without Directory Enquiries? Even though I didn't have the address of the Flamingo Motel in Malibu, I managed to persuade the nice young man on the other end of the phone to go through his lists for me, and bingo! So the hotel existed, at least. Next job was to call them. I had a momentary qualm about the size of my phone-bill next quarter, but I couldn't let that stop me now. I got through to Malibu at five o'clock that afternoon and the receptionist was enormously helpful in that eager American way, but couldn't remember an Englishwoman called Connie Trevor. There was nothing in the register, at any rate. Wait a minute, said the receptionist, I'll ask Adeline, and before I could protest, down went the phone and I heard the sound of lifted voices as Adeline was summoned. I hadn't mentioned I was calling from Belgium. I sat impatiently, listening to a conversation on the other side of the world and mentally clocking up the cost. But Adeline couldn't remember anyone English either, and she'd have been sure to know, because her husband Joe was from Scunthorpe and she always asked English people where they came from in case they came from Scunthorpe too. I don't know who was more disappointed: them or me.

If Connie'd flown to the US after her Italian holiday, there'd be a record somewhere of the ticket she'd booked. We had to find it. There was no way I could do that myself. I needed Luc Vanderauwera. I also had to tell him about the letter and get him to contact the British

137

police. They'd need to check the letter for fingerprints and get the handwriting analysed by experts. The trouble was, there was no way I could get in touch with him. I had to wait till he rang. If he ever did.

Women spend too much of their lives waiting. I paced up and down the apartment that night like a caged carnivore waiting for that phone call and wondering glumly if I was going to be confined to quarters for the whole week.

The phone rang at about nine o'clock. I leapt on it. A faint female voice said:

'Matilda?'

'Who's this?' I snapped.

'It's Ann. Ann Wilcox. Don't you remember?'

'Ann, where are you? Where've you been? Are you in England?'

'No, we're in Antwerp,' she said.

'Antwerp?' I had to sit down. What the hell was she doing in Antwerp?

'Look, Matilda, there's something I've got to tell you. I promised Nigel I wouldn't, but it's no use. I can't carry on like this. It's all my fault.'

'What is?'

There was a silence at the other end, but I thought I could hear the sound of sniffling.

'It's Connie's apartment,' she got out finally. 'You know it was broken into?'

'Yes,' I said impatiently.

'It was Nigel,' she said dolefully. 'He made a copy of Connie's keys during that fortnight when I was feeding Hortense. Then he went back and burgled the place. I didn't know till two days ago. But we were reading in the paper about how she'd disappeared, and he – he's terrified the police might think he had something to do with it, so he told me the whole story. What are we going to do?'

I sat staring at the wall with my mouth open. It was Nigel who'd burgled Connie's apartment! Until that moment I hadn't really believed that Nigel actually existed.

'Ann,' I said, 'where's Nigel now? Why haven't you gone back to England?'

'He never had any intention of going back,' Ann said miserably. 'And I couldn't go back without him. I cancelled my flight and we're staying with a friend of his here. He didn't want me to tell anyone, not even my family. It's horrible. I want to go home. I don't know what to do, so I called you. I thought you'd be able to suggest something.'

'The only thing is to persuade him to go to the police,' I said. 'If he tells them what he knows, they may go easy on him. Has he done this kind of thing before?'

'I don't know,' she said, still sniffling. 'I'll try and persuade him, Matilda. But suppose he won't? He's really scared. You know what the police are like here.'

'Then you'll have to go yourself,' I said. 'This isn't Turkey, you know. They're not as bad as all that.'

'I couldn't,' she said desperately. 'He'd never forgive me.'

'Listen,' I said. 'You can't seriously be thinking of staying with him now. First of all, he's a thief. He used you to get into Connie's apartment. And secondly, now you know, you could be implicated in the burglary too, not to mention Connie's disappearance.'

'But I love him,' she wailed, and I heard the sound of tears beginning in earnest.

It took me a minute or two to calm her down and I could only repeat what I'd already said: either she or Nigel had to go to the police about this.

'I suppose you're right,' she said, gulping. 'I'll try and talk to him. I really will try. Mat, will you promise not to tell anyone for the time being? At least for a few days.'

'OK,' I said. 'Tell me where you're staying.'

'I couldn't do that. Nigel would be furious.'

'Well, give me your phone number, at least,' I said impatiently. 'I've got to be able to contact you.'

She dithered for a moment or two, but finally gave me the number. I wrote it on the pad by the telephone and rang off. No wonder the English police had drawn a blank. How could Ann be such an idiot?

I didn't get much sleep that night and I don't know how I contained my impatience during the next couple of days, but there was no point wearing grooves in the parquet, so I finally decided to go about my normal business and to hell with the phone. On Wednesday, the agency rang. There was no work for the following week yet, but they were still looking. On Thursday I was out for most of the day. I got home around four and immediately the phone rang. I pounced on it. It was a friend reminding me that I'd promised to go and see the latest Arnold Schwarzenegger with her and would that evening do? I said 'Yes', grateful for some distraction, and arranged to meet her out at Kinepolis for a bite to eat and the late evening film. Then I got into the bath.

The bloody phone rang again immediately. I nearly killed myself leaping out, grabbed a towel and raced dripping into the living room to snatch the receiver. I heard the demented yakking of a public phone booth; then there was a metallic clatter, and a man's voice said: 'Matilda?'

I said. 'It's me.' There was a pool of water collecting on the floor.

'Luc,' he said. 'I haven't got much change here. Any news?'

'Loads,' I said. 'When can we talk?'

'I can't come round till tonight, late. Will you be home?'

'No, I'm going to Kinepolis.'

'You're always going somewhere,' he said with mild exasperation. 'OK, I'll pick you up there. What film are you seeing?'

'The Schwarzenegger. The last show; starts at nine.'

'OK. I'll see you tonight. Around eleven.'

'Fine,' I said. 'Take care.' The connection went dead in my hand.

So it was 'Matilda' and 'Luc' now, was it? For some odd reason, everything seemed to have got on track again. I leapt back in the bath and burst into song, feeling ridiculously light-hearted. I was looking forward to my evening now.

Kinepolis is an entertainment complex out by the Heysel stadium in the north-west of town. It has twenty-eight cinemas and is doing great business. I took the métro out to Heysel and met my friend Chrissie for a quick *croque-monsieur* before the show. We got chatted up in the café; Chrissie is a left-over from the punk era and attracts a lot of attention. My short skirt seemed to find favour with the punters too.

The film was a typical Schwarzenegger vehicle: long on special effects and short on plot and characterization: but Chrissie and I are both devoted fans of Arnie's, so we didn't mind. You don't, after all, go to a Schwarzenegger film if you want culture. I was in such an exhilarated mood that Chrissie asked if I was taking anything and looked disbelieving when I said I wasn't. When I told her I was meeting a friend after the film, she grinned and said he must be something special if I was looking forward to it so much. That stopped me in my tracks. Just why was I looking forward to it so much? I'm not interested in married policemen. Keep cool, Matilda.

Chrissie left me outside the cinema and as her multi-coloured hair disappeared into the crowd, I caught a grip on myself and tried to conjure up a businesslike frame of mind. But when I saw Luc emerge from the crowd and come towards me, I felt a sudden rush of warmth and gave him such a welcoming smile that three people turned to stare. He was carrying his jacket over his shoulder and looked as if he hadn't slept for a week. To my utter astonishment, he came right up and kissed my cheek, just as if we really were long-standing friends meeting casually after a film. I felt his hand on my bare arm and shivered. It was the first time he had touched me.

'Come on,' he said. 'Let's get out of here. What have you been up to?'

The car was miles away. As we picked our way across the unpaved car-park, I started telling him everything that had happened since Saturday night, which seemed like a hundred years ago: my talk with Terry Evans, Linda's bombshell about the letter, and my absolute conviction that it couldn't have come from Connie and why.

We reached the car and he opened the passenger door and held it for me. I heard the familiar crackle of the

141

radio as I got in. I pulled my blasted skirt down as far as it would go. Suddenly I seemed to have too much leg showing. Luc threw his jacket in the back of the car, got in and slammed the door. He turned towards me.

'I don't have much to report,' he said. 'I got hold of the chap in Australia, but he couldn't add very much to what we already know.'

It was probably evidence of a mean character, but I felt a faint glow of satisfaction that his enquiries had been no more successful than mine. I tried to hide it. I must have succeeded, because he went on without a break: 'And I've drawn a total blank on Ann Wilcox and her boyfriend.'

I can't explain why I said what I did next, except that I was probably carried away on a wave of warmth and confidence and didn't stop to think.

'They're in Antwerp,' I said. 'She called me. It was Nigel who burgled Connie's apartment. He'd made a copy of her keys.'

Then I stopped dead, remembering my promise. Damn. The Haycastle big mouth.

'Oh, had he?' Luc said softly. Then he looked at my face. 'What's the matter?'

'I promised not to say anything for a few days, till she's had a chance to persuade him to go to the police.'

Luc laughed. 'She'll be lucky. Where in Antwerp?'

'I don't know the address. But surely it's unlikely he had anything to do with Connie vanishing. If I'm right, and the letter is a hoax, then it seems most likely that this friend Connie was going to stay with in Brussels is responsible for her disappearance.'

'So it would seem,' Luc said. 'Or at least, he or she would have been the last person to see Connie alive and could shed more light on the matter.'

'And I think it's Graham Ferguson,' I finished.

'Does he have a flat in the Tomberg area? Did you check the phone book?'

'Yes. Nothing. But that doesn't mean a thing. It wouldn't necessarily be listed.'

142

'There's no proof,' he said. 'It's all circumstantial.'

'The letter might tell us something. And we ought to check the flights to the US the week Connie disappeared. And as for the Tomberg clue, there's always the register of leases, or the *maison communale*.'

He gave me a look in which amusement was struggling with exasperation.

'You're enjoying this,' he said. 'Have you ever thought of joining the police?'

'No,' I said truthfully. 'Will you do it?'

'OK. I can check the US flights easily enough. And I'll get on to the UK police about the letter. In the meantime, you stick close to Ferguson. If you keep on rattling his cage, maybe he'll give something away. Anything else?'

I shook my head.

'Well, let's go on back to town and get a drink.'

He started the car and switched the lights on.

I said, rather gloomily: 'We're going to look really silly if Connie turns up after all this.'

'I don't think Connie's going to turn up ever again,' Luc said grimly. 'I've got a bad feeling about this whole thing. Call it policeman's instinct, if you like. The whole affair smells.'

I said nothing. I'd had the same feeling for days.

We'd reached the Gare du Nord area, travelling at Luc's usual headlong speed. Suddenly the radio squawked and a man's voice rapped something out in Flemish. I didn't understand, but Luc leaned forward, snatched the intercom and spoke into it. As he replaced the thing, I said: 'What is it?'

'Call for assistance,' he said briefly. 'Hang on.'

If I'd thought we were travelling fast before, I rapidly discovered that I was wrong. Wrenching the car round, Luc sent it racing down a side-street and round several corners. Pedestrians leapt for their lives. I closed my eyes and hung on to the seat. Then, equally suddenly, we screeched to a stop. I heard him snap: 'Stay here!' The door opened and I unclosed my eyes in time to see him sprinting towards a group of men who were struggling together on the pavement outside a closed and shuttered shop.

We were in the mass of dark, run-down streets between the Place Sainte Catherine and the canal. A patrol car stood nearby, doors wide open, light flashing. A policeman's cap lay on the ground. There was a lot of noise: men's voices yelling, the crash of breaking glass, the throbbing of the police siren. I suddenly heard more sirens in the distance; as I watched, a couple of youths broke away from the scrap and sprinted off down an alley. The mêlée broke apart; in alarm, I suddenly saw that two of the men had Luc by the arms, while a third was laying into him inexpertly but savagely with his fists. I realized that Luc wasn't carrying his gun and I started to scramble out of the car in a panic. Luc kicked out, and the attacker swore, drew off and pulled out a knife. I saw it quite clearly, even in that dim light, at that distance.

I think I must have gone quite crazy. I yelled out Luc's name and charged full-tilt at the group, still yelling like a banshee. It was probably the most dangerous thing I've ever done in my life. I had no weapon; I know almost nothing about self-defence; I had no very clear idea of what I was going to do when I reached them. But to my great good fortune, my rashness surprised them as much as it had me. The action faltered and stopped; four amazed faces turned gaping. They were pale, featureless blurs to me. Then Luc, the first to recover his wits, lunged out desperately and managed to land a kick on the arm holding the knife. The blade leapt up in the air in my direction. I skidded to a halt in alarm, and the knife clattered on the cobblestones not six inches from my foot. I took a wild swiping kick at it, half-missing, and the horrible thing skittered sideways into the gutter.

I saw Luc wrench himself free and follow up his kick with a knee in the stomach and a most professional-looking short jab; his assailant doubled up with a scream, hands to his nose. The sirens were right on top of us now. I'm not quite sure what happened after that, but the noise seemed to die down and the fight came slowly to a stop.

Uniforms and flashing lights surrounded us. I saw that the shutters of the shop had been smashed; there were bits of wood lying around on the pavement among the garbage. A crowd began to gather, now that it was all over. I was shaking violently. Then Luc's arm was round me, steadyingly. He was breathing fast, but didn't seem to be visibly damaged. Voices were talking loudly in Flemish. I heard Luc answering, still holding me. Somebody patted my arm and said something jovial and congratulatory. They all seemed to be very pleased with themselves. A van drove up and half a dozen men were herded unceremoniously into it. One was bleeding buckets from the nose. The van drove off, followed by one of the police cars. There were more handshakings and cheery farewells in Flemish, then Luc said: 'I'm taking you home.'

In the car, he reached into the back seat for his jacket and put it round me. I felt the heaviness of the gun in one pocket. I was still shaking.

'I'm sorry. I can't stop,' I said.

'It's shock,' he replied. 'You'll be OK.'

Then he said: 'Next time, stay in the car.'

I looked at him with a sudden flash of indignation at his ingratitude, but then I saw he was smiling, so I abandoned my angry retort, leaned back and closed my eyes.

Chapter 18

I didn't open them again until we were home, by which time I had stopped shivering. Neither of us had said anything. When Luc cut the engine, there was a deep silence. I opened my eyes and saw that he was looking at me with a strange expression on his face.

I knew what he was going to do before he did it. I think I moved towards him in the same instant as he reached out for me. I'd forgotten how uncomfortable it is to kiss in cars. He lifted his mouth from mine for an instant to change his grip on me and I thought my bones would break under his hands. My shirt was already out of my waistband and my skirt had ridden up as far as it would go.

We got out of the car somehow and into the lift. I was jammed into the corner and he was kissing me as if that were the only thing left to do in the world. His hands were all over me. Thank heaven nobody saw us. I have never wanted a man so much. It was just as well, because by the time we got into the flat, I couldn't have stopped him, even if I'd wanted to. We had just about enough sense left to take the necessary safety measures; after that, common sense and reason just went out of the window. We hardly spoke, except to say each other's names; it was too urgent, too desperate. Almost my last coherent thought was that I should have known it would be all or nothing with us; we'd been quarrelling like lovers ever since we met.

I woke up suddenly in the middle of the night to find myself alone in the bed. My head was perfectly clear.

With an almost supernatural lucidity, the evening's events passed through my mind like a silent film. Oh God, Matilda, what have you done? He's a married man. He's in the police. You don't know anything about him at all. You must be out of your head. My brave speech to Georges sprang, word-perfect, into my mind and I groaned out loud. I should have kept my mouth shut. I thought of Jeff Barnes's proposition and my virtuous refusal. I thought of Aaron. I thought of Giulia's shivery little laugh.

I hadn't heard Luc leave. I got up, aching unaccustomedly, for we hadn't been gentle with one another, and switched on the bedside light. Luc's clothes were all over the floor, together with mine. He hadn't gone, then. I put on a dressing-gown and went into the bathroom. In the mirror I looked the way you're supposed to after heavy sex.

Luc was sitting at the kitchen table, a glass of water in front of him, looking at it with the expression of a man who is thinking hard. He had his jeans on. There were bruises beginning on his chest and arms, from the fight. Hortense was sitting on the table, one leg hoisted in the air, washing.

I really had no idea what to expect. Men are odd. Sometimes they have nothing to say, afterwards. They just want to get away as soon as possible.

Luc looked up quickly as I came in, then stretched an arm out. I went to him; and, still sitting, he put both arms right around me and held me close, his face against my body. I couldn't help myself. I held him tightly, one hand in his rough brown hair and the other arm round his shoulders. It was a couple of moments before we loosened our grip on one another.

He said quietly: 'There are things I've got to tell you.'

It only takes a few minutes to describe a spoiled life. He spoke quietly and unmelodramatically and I listened, aching with pity, sitting at the table with him. He had married Marie-Paule under the impression that she was two months pregnant with his child; in reality, she was

147

three months pregnant with someone else's. He'd begun to suspect even before the birth, when the dates didn't seem to be matching the original forecasts. When the baby was born, a patently normal, full-term child, Luc was jovially told by the obstetrician that Marie-Paule must have got her dates wrong.

No one else seemed to suspect anything. Her family fell over themselves to make things easy for the young couple. A house that had belonged to a recently deceased aunt was made over to them; Luc's career in the police force received a number of subtle boosts, thanks to his father-in-law's influence. As luck would have it, the child Daniel resembled Marie-Paule; there was no evidence to be seen there. There was only a poisonous suspicion that was nearly a certainty.

The marriage wasn't a success. How could it be? Three bitter, disruptive years later, Luc found out that Marie-Paule was having an affair with a married friend of theirs: Olivier, a member of the football team he'd belonged to before his marriage. As usual with such things, everyone knew except him. There was a confrontation, and Marie-Paule, beside herself with spite, threw in his face that Daniel was Olivier's child, and that the affair had been going on for years. Her family had known all along. Luc told me quite dispassionately that, at that moment, he'd wanted to beat Marie-Paule into oblivion, to blot her out of the life that she'd poisoned. It had been the child's frightened face that had stopped him.

Marie Paule had wanted a divorce. Bitterly humiliated, vindictive, determined to punish her, he'd refused. Her family supported him, appalled at the idea of a scandal.

'It was the stupidest thing I've ever done,' he told me, his voice quiet and empty. 'I wanted to make her suffer, but I only hurt myself worse in the process.' He hadn't touched Marie-Paule since that day. He hadn't touched any woman for five years, he told me. He was determined to give his wife no chance to shake him off. And, in any case, the women he met sickened him. They all seemed to have her face, her perfume, her tricks of smiling and flirting and lying. He couldn't bear it.

So he stayed, sharing the house with a woman who'd become a stranger and a child that wasn't his own. He did well in the police at first, but recently, he had acquired a reputation for being arrogant and rash, too ready to take risks, too quick to volunteer for the really dangerous assignments. He'd had some narrow escapes. He'd made enemies. And that was how it had been, he said, till the day he walked into my apartment.

'And there you were, *ma belle Mathilde*,' he said, with a slight smile, 'bloody-minded as hell and not about to let anyone push you around. Ready to follow me into those sewers, where I had no business to take you. Ready to do anything at all to find out what's happened to somebody you didn't even know. The air is clear around you, Matilda. Lies can't survive. What was it that little reptile said about you?'

' "Pack up your holy purity and wheel it out of my house",' I quoted obligingly.

He laughed wryly. 'That was it. Holy purity.'

'You make me sound like a virgin saint,' I said, getting up. 'I'm neither.'

'I know.' He reached out and pulled me towards him by the belt of the dressing-gown. 'You were so beautiful in your red dress the other night. I hadn't realized how beautiful, till then. I wanted you. It was like a wall falling down.'

His hands were already engaged under the loosened dressing-gown. I put out my arm and switched the kitchen light off.

'The neighbours have all got binoculars,' I murmured.

That's the understatement of the millenium. When the moon's full, they've got infra-red vision.

When I woke up, it was full daylight and he was sitting on the edge of the bed, already dressed.

'*Liefje*, I have to go,' he said.

I sat up in sudden alarm.

'I've got a lot of things to sort out,' he said. 'Is it all right if I come back tonight?'

'All right?' I echoed. 'You'd better damn well come back tonight.'

149

He smiled, but I could see it was an effort. He looked desperately tired. I suppose I did too. He had a piece of paper in his hand.

'These are all my phone numbers. Home, office, and my mother's number in Lier. But don't call my home unless it's an emergency.'

I nodded. He hugged me very tightly and left. I heard the front door close.

Hortense looked in with an urgent mew. She wanted her breakfast.

I felt absolutely exhausted. Why don't these things ever happen at weekends? Thank heaven, at least I didn't have to go to the office and pretend to be working. I crawled out of bed. A cup of coffee and a hot bath helped a little. I still couldn't really believe what had happened. I thought of Aaron, with considerable wryness. That was an unprofitable line of thought, however.

I thought I ought to ring Georges and was about to pick up the phone, when he rang me. Thought transference, he said. He hadn't anything to report yet concerning Ferguson, but he was still hoping. He asked how things were going at my end and I gave him all the news concerning Connie. I was brief about Luc; I didn't feel equal to giving Georges a detailed explanation on that score. But Georges reads minds, even on the telephone.

'Do I take it that you and your crusader have, how shall I put it, discovered the Holy Grail?' he asked.

My silence must have been answer enough. A brief suspicion flashed through my mind that this had been the purpose of his call. I wondered suddenly whether Georges had really had a late appointment the previous Saturday night.

'There is no need for bashfulness,' Georges said, satisfaction in his voice. 'You are entitled to a little pleasure now and then.'

His tone made me a little sharp.

'I'm glad you approve,' I said. 'He might be around for a long time.'

This time the silence was at Georges' end. When he

replied, I was startled at the alarm in his voice.

'Matilda, I can see that he is attractive, and there is after all no reason why you should not sleep with him if you wish, but you are not, I hope, proposing to begin a serious relationship with him?'

He sounded really disturbed.

'Why ever not?' I asked.

'Firstly, he is married, with a child– '

'It's not his child,' I interrupted. 'He's told me all about that. He doesn't get on with his wife.'

I distinctly heard Georges groan, and despite myself, I flushed. It is, after all, the standard married man's excuse. My wife doesn't understand me.

'Matilda, I have taken the trouble to make investigations about your Inspector Vanderauwera. I am not saying that he does not mean what he tells you, but just consider. Nine years of an unhappy, broken marriage. A record of risk-taking and rash exploits. He has alienated people, made enemies. Those things are the mark of an unstable personality. You will be taking too great a risk. It is far too dangerous.'

'You're wrong, Georges. It's all the other way round. He's the one who's suffered.'

'You know him so well, after one night?' Georges said gently.

After I'd put the phone down, I walked up and down, thinking. There were too many things all mixed in together. I was too tired. My mind was in a daze after the various emotional and physical shocks of the previous night. I couldn't straighten out all the different threads. From the back of my mind resurfaced all the doubts about a relationship of any kind with a married policeman. My thoughts went this way and that, uselessly.

Luc had been honest about his marriage; on the other hand, he hadn't said anything to indicate that his feelings for me weren't just a passing fancy. The night had been astonishingly, passionately intense; but after all, he hadn't slept with any woman for five years. For that matter, I hadn't said anything either; on the point of muttering something irrevocable several times during the night, I had kept it to myself, out of a strange desire not to burden him with emotions that maybe he couldn't reciprocate.

Sex is a strange thing. Sometimes, it means no more to you than a casual conversation. Sometimes it changes your life. Deep down I had the rather hollow feeling that this had changed mine. I didn't know him well enough to know whether it had changed his.

It was no good. I was too tired to think. I sat down on the sofa for a couple of minutes and fell asleep, just like that. The shrilling of the telephone woke me up, confused and shaken, hours later. It was Ann Wilcox, hysterical.

'How could you, Matilda, how could you? You promised you wouldn't say anything. How could you?'

I could only manage to get out: 'What's happened? Tell me what's happened.'

'Nigel's been arrested. The police have just taken him away. I trusted you, Matilda. How could you do this to me?'

And on the telephone table right under my nose was the writing-pad with the Antwerp phone number on it. The number that Luc must have noted down before he left that morning.

Chapter 19

Luc walked in around eight o'clock that evening, looking exhausted. I was exhausted too. I'd spent the intervening time in a stew of doubt and confusion. A confrontation was the last thing either of us needed, but I couldn't think of a way round it.

I don't believe in pussyfooting around.

'You had Nigel Grant arrested,' I said, and he stopped dead and looked at me, the shadows deep under his eyes. He didn't bother to deny it or even to ask how I knew. Instead he said:

'I had to. I needed to get myself back on the case officially and this was the only way. And he'd never have gone to the police of his own accord. That type never does.'

'You might at least have given him the chance,' I said tightly. 'I promised to give Ann time to persuade him. Now she thinks I'm the one who shopped him.'

'I'm sorry,' he said, sitting down heavily on the sofa and closing his eyes. 'I'm really sorry, Matilda. But it was necessary. If we want to find Connie, we've got to question him.'

'Was that why you came back here last night, to get the phone number?'

That made him open his eyes again. He stared at me sombrely. 'No,' he said. 'You know it wasn't. Or I wouldn't be here now.'

'Why are you here?' I asked.

'Because I think I love you.'

It wasn't much of a declaration, but he was too tired

for romance. I came slowly to the sofa and sat down by him.

'Sorry,' he said, taking my hand. 'I know it's rather sudden.'

'Last night was rather sudden,' I said. 'Are you sure?'

'Yes,' he said simply. 'How about you?'

'Me too,' I said.

To hell with Georges.

Love doesn't thrive if you're tired and hungry, so I sent him off for a hot shower while I put together a simple meal. When it was ready, I went to tell him and found him asleep on my bed, his hands folded on his chest like a carving on a tomb. It seemed a pity to wake him up.

The food revived him. While we ate, he told me about the day's events. The Connie Trevor investigation had been reopened and he'd been told to get on with it. The Antwerp police had found Nigel and made the actual arrest. Luc was going up the next day to talk to the culprit, who was being held in connection with a number of house break-ins in Antwerp.

'The police in the UK are checking out the letter, but I've no idea how long it'll take. They say they've got other priorities. The standard excuse. And I faxed a picture of Connie to the police in Malibu and asked them to make official investigations at the motel, just in case. In the meantime the airlines have checked their computer system and confirmed that no one called Connie Trevor flew to the US or anywhere else from Brussels in June. They're checking departures from other western European cities as well. So far, I'd say your feeling was right.'

I got up to make the coffee. He was watching me with a look that I was beginning to recognize. I suddenly remembered the specific events of the previous evening and felt myself shiver. There was always that edge of violence about him. It was deeply sexy. Giulia, more immediately responsive to men's sexual presence than I, had seen it at once. Georges, the epitome of civilized refinement, had seen it too. So had I, now. I turned and looked straight at Luc. He got up slowly and moved towards me. I felt that deep shiver again. Coming close, he took my face in his hands and studied it.

'Those eyes,' he murmured. 'I've never seen eyes as clear as yours. Warrior's eyes, like swords.'

I closed them as he bent to kiss me.

The next morning, over coffee, he said casually: 'I've been making plans. As soon as we've got this case cracked, I'm resigning from the police. I've taken enough aggravation from my father-in-law. And I've spoken to my lawyer about a divorce.'

I took a deep breath. This was a man who didn't hang about.

'Are you sure you want to?' I asked.

'Yes,' he said. 'I've wasted enough of my life. If I don't make a change now, I never will.'

'Will your wife go along?'

'I think I can persuade her. She'll probably be glad to be rid of me.'

'What about Daniel?' I ventured somewhat hesitantly. I had a feeling that this was an unknown and potentially problematic area.

His face was sombre. 'I'll have to pay child support. Even if he isn't mine, he's been living under my roof for nine years. Anyway, none of it's his fault. He's just an innocent bystander.'

'Do you get on well with him?'

'I hardly know him,' Luc said with a sigh. 'I've never been able to communicate with him. He's very quiet, very withdrawn. Lives in a world of his own. He'll hardly miss me, I think. I hope not.'

He went off early, leaving me with the unenviable task of pursuing the Ferguson enquiry. I was dressing, trying to decide whether to call Julian Wychell or perhaps take the whole thing by the scruff of the neck and contact Vibeke direct, when the doorbell rang.

'It's Julian,' said the voice over the entryphone. 'May I come up?'

Luckily I'd got my clothes more or less on. He was

looking exceedingly smart in a well-cut grey business suit and brilliant white shirt.

'I thought it was Saturday,' I said, blinking. Maybe we'd skipped a day.

'It is, but running your own show is a seven-day-a-week affair. I had a business appointment this morning. I came to ask if you're doing anything for lunch. I know a place where we can eat in the garden and it's a shame to waste such lovely weather. And we can discuss the organization of the next event.'

I'd been planning to go downtown and buy a present for some friends who were getting married soon, but who am I to refuse a free lunch?

'I'd love to,' I said, smiling. 'But I'll have to change. I can't go in jeans.'

'Go ahead. I'll wait.'

Sitting under a parasol in a little Italian garden, with a fountain plashing gently behind me and scores of waiters attending to my every whim, I regretted for a brief moment that it wasn't Luc sitting opposite me, smiling over a glass of chilled Sancerre. I wasn't going to let it stop me enjoying lunch, though. If I couldn't have Luc, this pleasant man was an agreeable second best.

'So what's the next event?' I asked. 'Not more Renaissance music, I hope.'

'No. A festival of European folk-dances,' he said.

I groaned. 'People jumping about with bells in their hands?'

'We do have some genuine English morris-dancers coming, yes,' he said, laughing. 'Also groups from other European countries. I'm off to Germany tonight to talk to some people there about it and I wanted to see you first. I was hoping you'd help me organize this, rather than just selling programmes or helping behind the bar.'

'I'm flattered,' I said. I was. He explained what would be involved – mostly telephone calls and a bit of correspondence.

'Who else is involved?' I asked casually.

'The usual bunch. Graham and Vibeke, Françoise, various people you don't know yet. We'll have a meeting when I get back and I'll introduce you.'

I suddenly saw a way of preparing the ground for my next approach to Ferguson.

'I'm afraid Graham's gone off me a bit,' I said, with what I hoped sounded like an embarrassed laugh. 'I may have offended him at the concert the other night.'

'Offended Graham? Surely not?'

'Well, I haven't exactly been his flavour of the month since all that business about Connie Trevor. It did seem to upset him rather.'

I wondered if I were sounding a little too ingenuous, but Julian seemed to take it at face value.

'Of course he was upset,' he said. 'Anybody would be, to be told that someone they knew had disappeared. It's only natural.'

'Well, maybe you could give Graham a message from me?' I said. 'I heard from the police that the enquiry's been called off. Apparently Connie's turned up safe and sound in the US. Her sister had a letter from her. So we can all stop worrying.'

'That is good news,' he exclaimed. 'I'm sure Graham will be delighted. And don't worry about offending him. He's not the type who offends easily.'

I wasn't sure he was right in this case, but I wasn't about to contradict him.

The scampi in raspberry vinegar had been delicious. I sat back with a sigh. The garden was full of flowers, and a light breeze was blowing, just enough to prevent the heat from becoming unbearable. Julian had taken off his jacket, which is as far as an English businessman goes in public. If he'd been American, he'd have been wearing a short-sleeved shirt, but that wasn't cricket. Somebody refilled my glass.

'Enough business,' Julian said. 'The weather's too good. I've just realized I don't know a thing about you. Tell me about yourself.'

I gave him the potted Haycastle history, same as I'd given Aaron. In the meantime, chicken arrived, grilled in

157

ginger, mangetout peas arranged in a fan shape above and below.

'Now you,' I said.

'Winchester, Cambridge, five years in the UK, three years in practice here, nine in the Commission, and the last three or so as a consultant. Belgian wife, two adorable children, Clare and Sebastian, loads of rather less adorable Belgian relatives by marriage.' He stopped and laughed. 'How's that?'

'Cursory,' I said. 'I take it your wife comes from a big family?'

'Not only big, but influential.' He stopped and made a slight grimace. 'I can't deny it's been useful in business here, but all the same, there are a lot of problems inherent in mixed marriages. I sometimes wonder if I made the right choice.'

'It can be difficult,' I agreed, thinking of various mixed nationality couples I know. 'In my experience, English people tend to find Belgian family life rather stifling.'

'That's only too true. And Françoise is very attached to her family – terrific sense of duty. It's very laudable, I know, but it's hard to live with. It all seems to have reached a crescendo just recently.'

'Perhaps she should ease up on all these extra activities?' I suggested.

'That might be one way to take the pressure off. She's going to the Ardennes this weekend – we have a place down there. The rest will do her good. But I don't want to heap all my worries on you. It's too beautiful a day and I'm enjoying myself too much. Tell me what you like doing in the evenings. Didn't you say you liked the opera?'

We were chatting away like old mates when I heard a voice I recognized. It seems impossible to do anything in Brussels without being spotted by somebody you don't want to see. How Connie'd managed to keep her affair a secret for so long, I really don't know. This time, hell and damnation, it was Isabelle Lefèvre. She was beautifully turned out in a beige linen suit and the usual heavy-gauge jewellery, and was with a girl-friend from the hand of the same doll-maker. She ignored me, greeted Julian, and launched into enthusiastic small-talk, while her friend hovered uncertainly, balancing on the grass with difficulty in very high-heeled shoes. Julian was politely unencouraging and finally Isabelle gave up and allowed the head waiter to lead her to a table some way off. Julian breathed a sigh of relief and cast a comical look up at the sky.

'Thank goodness. I thought she'd never go away. I couldn't help noticing that you two don't seem to be getting on and I didn't want our lunch spoiled.'

'She doesn't like me much,' I admitted. 'I don't know why. I've hardly exchanged two words with her. Just one of those things, I suppose.'

Looking over my shoulder, I saw that Isabelle was staring at us with a queer look on her face. Her girl-friend said something and she replied pettishly and picked up the menu with an ill-tempered flounce.

Time passed. We were at the dessert stage. As our ice-cream appeared, a waiter made his way to our table, bent and whispered discreetly in Julian's ear. He put his napkin on the table with a slight look of annoyance.

'There's a phone call for me,' he said. 'Please excuse me, Matilda. Don't wait – the ice-cream will melt.'

He followed the waiter into the dim interior of the restaurant. I sat happily, lulled by sunshine and white wine, rather dreamily absorbing nut and honey ice-cream. The garden was full of the murmur of bees and diners. I wondered how Luc was getting on in Antwerp. Probably eating a tired tuna mayonnaise sandwich with indigestible coffee in a hot police station somewhere. I thought about Luc longingly for a minute or two. Julian's ice-cream was melting rapidly. A waiter noticed, tut-tutted, and removed it, promising to bring another. That call was taking a long time.

It was a good ten minutes before Julian reappeared, followed by the waiter with the fresh dessert.

'I am sorry,' Julian exclaimed as he sat down. 'It took much longer than I expected. I hope you weren't bored.'

I disclaimed, and watched him eat his dessert, which he did with the frank enjoyment of a small boy. As the waiters brought coffee, I saw Isabelle Lefèvre emerge from inside the restaurant, putting on her dark-glasses as the sunlight fell on her face. I thought for a moment that she was going to approach us again, but she went straight back to her own table. I breathed a sigh of relief.

We didn't finish lunch till three; obviously Julian didn't have any business appointments that afternoon. As he called for the bill, I made my way into the gloom of the restaurant, searched with some difficulty for the ladies' room, which was all marble and gilt and mirrors, and started to repair my make-up. My nose was glowing like a beacon. Then the door banged and I looked up at the mirror to see Isabelle Lefèvre behind me, her eyes very bright blue in the artificial light. I turned, powder compact in hand.

'You think you're so clever,' she said, her whole face tight with vindictiveness. 'So very clever.'

Men really have no idea of the dramatic events that take place in ladies' rooms.

I have to say that I gawped. Isabelle said impatiently: 'Oh, don't pretend you don't know what I'm talking about. Julian! You've been running after him from the minute you set eyes on him. Well, let me tell you you're wasting your time. He's taken.'

'That's interesting,' I said. 'By whom?'

'Me. And don't think you can muscle in and push me out, either. He's mine.'

'Let me get this right,' I said carefully. 'Are you trying to tell me that you're having an affair with Julian Wychell? Or are you just hoping to?'

She turned to the mirror and tossed her long hair back with a triumphant expression.

'Oh, we're having an affair all right,' she said to my mirror image. 'If you don't believe me, you can go and ask Françoise. She knows.'

Françoise?

'His wife knows?' I asked cautiously. This was beginning to sound like an episode of *Dynasty*. I wondered

160

briefly what Isabelle had between her ears. My money was on polystyrene packing chips.

'She knows a lot of things, that one,' Isabelle said, leaning towards her own reflection and smoothing a perfectly groomed eyebrow. 'She doesn't care, as long as he's discreet. She knows he only married her for the money.'

'I don't believe you,' I said flatly.

'Then you're a fool,' she said, turning towards me. 'There are lots of things you don't know about Julian. For instance, he knew that woman who disappeared – that Connie person.'

'He's never even met her,' I said.

'That's what you think.' She turned back to the mirror, the triumphant smile on her lips again.

My hand shot out and grabbed her thin wrist so hard that all her bracelets jingled and she gave a gasp of pain.

'What do you know about Julian and Connie Trevor?' I asked fiercely.

Voices sounded outside the door. My grip relaxed involuntarily and Isabelle twisted herself free, shot into one of the loos and bolted the door. A moment later, two large Flemish ladies sailed in, bringing with them a dense fall-out of heavy perfume.

Damn it!

Outside in the corridor, I stopped to think. I have to admit I was shaken. Could it be true? Or was Isabelle making it all up for some petty neurotic reason of her own? I just couldn't credit it. Julian's behaviour towards her had never given the least indication that they were sleeping together – there's always some fatal gesture or tone of voice that gives lovers away. Intimacy can't be hidden. I trusted Julian. And anyway, I wouldn't take Isabelle Lefèvre's opinion about the time of day, so why should I believe her about this?

Unsurprisingly, I was rather uncommunicative going home. I kept looking sideways at the serene profile beside me and listening to the untroubled voice talking about this and that, and I couldn't bring myself to believe what I'd just heard. It wasn't possible.

Julian dropped me at the flat with a cheerful reminder

that he'd be in touch when he got back from Germany, and drove off with a wave and a smile. Inside, I found Hortense asleep on the sofa. Pensively, I got down beside her and began to stroke the fur between her ears. Her eyes didn't open, but the tip of her tail started to twitch irritably. I desisted. I knew the danger signs now.

Then the phone rang. Luc. With, as usual, not so much as a hello. He sounded triumphant.

'All the bets are off,' he said. 'You can forget the Ferguson investigation. We're on to a lead here. It looks as if Nigel Grant's responsible for Connie's disappearance after all.'

Chapter 20

I listened, speechless, while he elucidated.

'The Antwerp police searched the flat where he was bunking up. They found a number of Connie's bits and pieces – china, jewellery and so on. He hadn't had time to get rid of it all. They also found a sports bag he'd used to put the loot in, and there was a bloodstained towel in it. There was a lot of blood, and it's Connie's blood-group. We've been questioning Nigel Grant and his friends all day, but so far, nothing. He's admitted to burgling Connie's apartment, but he won't say any more.'

'But doesn't he have an explanation?' I asked, unbelieving.

'He says he just picked up the bag and shoved the stuff into it and didn't know there was a towel in it at all.'

'But that's perfectly plausible,' I said. Every sentence in my mind started with BUT.

'Not to me,' Luc said shortly. 'It's the nearest we've come to a genuine lead since the enquiry started. We're treating it as murder now. I'm staying up here till we get him to talk. He will. We've been leaning on him hard, and I reckon he'll come up with the goods before long.'

'But why should he have killed Connie?'

'That's what we're going to find out. Maybe she came back unexpectedly and caught him in the act. He's the type that would panic easily. I'll have to get the forensic people to go over Connie's flat again.'

'But what about the letter?' I said.

'Nigel could just as well have sent it as anyone else,' Luc said impatiently. 'I'll call you if there's any news.'

BUT, I said to myself as I put the phone down. What about Ferguson? What about Terry Evans? And what about Isabelle's revelations? I'd been in such a daze at Luc's news that I hadn't even told him about those. In any case, with his nose hot on Nigel's trail, he'd probably have discounted them all out of hand. But I wasn't prepared to ignore any lead, improbable or not. I'd already made my mind up what I was going to do. There was just one way to find out who was telling the truth. Crazy as it sounded, I was going to follow Isabelle's suggestion. I was going to ask Françoise.

With that resolution in mind, I spent a peaceful night, out of which I was shocked early in the morning by the urgent sound of the phone yet again. For the millionth time, I considered getting one of those phones that purr rather than shrill. But Hortense might get jealous and try to kill it.

It was Luc.

What, again?

'Nigel's in hospital,' he said, grim-voiced. 'He tried to commit suicide during the night.'

I couldn't believe my ears.

'It's not possible!' I protested, stunned. 'How on earth could he?'

'He tried to hang himself with his own shirt. He was alone in the cell and there was a double bunk with a metal framework. Fortunately somebody looked in and saw him in time. He didn't make a very good job of it – just good enough for him to be transferred to a clinic. He'll be all right, but I'll have to stay up here till he's recovered enough for me to question him.'

Everything derogatory I'd ever heard about the competence of the Belgian police came into my mind, but luckily I was still too stunned to say anything.

Luc went on: 'This just confirms my feeling that he's hiding the truth about Connie. He'd never have tried to kill himself if he'd only committed burglary.'

'Maybe he's just afraid of being locked up by foreign police in a strange country?' I suggested. It was my turn to sound grim. I didn't say that maybe Luc had leaned on him a little too hard, but it was in my mind.

If I'd felt guilty about Ann and Nigel before, I felt doubly so now. Could Luc be right? Had Connie come back unexpectedly and found Nigel peacefully burgling her apartment? Nobody'd heard or seen anything, and there had been no signs of a struggle. Assuming, of course, that the police had looked for signs of a struggle. And what would he have done with the body?

Get on with the investigation, Matilda.

I drove round to the Wychell house, which proved to be a very large detached mansion, in the more select reaches of Uccle. I drove up the gravel drive, parked, and knocked boldly on the front door. A pleasant middle-aged woman answered: the housekeeper. I explained that I needed to talk to Françoise urgently – a matter to do with the festival I was helping to organize. Monsieur Wychell, of course, was out of the country, so I couldn't contact him.

'I'm so sorry, but Madame is in the Ardennes,' the housekeeper said apologetically, and I suddenly remembered that Wychell had told me that himself at lunch.

'She has a small place near St Hubert and she goes down when she wants to relax,' the housekeeper went on. 'She's been so tired recently, she thought the break would do her good.'

'Is she on her own?'

'Yes, for once. Monsieur is in Germany and the children are at the coast. She doesn't get much time to herself. Such a busy life.'

'Do you have the phone number?'

'There's no telephone – it's just a hunting cabin really. Madame likes to be completely undisturbed when she goes down. But I expect her back in a couple of days' time.'

I wasn't prepared to wait that long. I wanted this matter cleared up as soon as possible.

'I'm afraid it's really urgent,' I said. 'Can you tell me how to get there?'

She was very obliging. I found myself in what was obviously the Wychells' office, while she got out the Ordnance Survey map of the area, made a photocopy of the relevant bit and carefully drew the route on it in fluorescent pen. By the look of it, the cabin was bang in the middle of pine forests and the roads were scarcely worthy of the name. I'd have to be careful not to get lost once I was off the motorway. I thanked the helpful lady, and got back into the car.

I considered for a moment before starting out. I was dressed for the city, in a summer dress and light sandals. The gear wasn't exactly suitable for orienteering, but I couldn't be bothered to go home and change. I found a garage, filled the car up and set straight off down the Namur motorway. It was another hot day. The motorway was packed with holiday traffic: big German cars whizzing up the fast lane and Dutch caravans in the slow lane blocking everyone's way. The entire Dutch nation takes to the road in the summer, taking all its provisions with it so as not to have to spend money on holiday. You should hear the French restaurateurs going on about them. I remembered, with a smile, Georges' joke about how you get fifty Dutchmen in a telephone kiosk. The answer is: you throw in a *dubbeltje*, which is a Dutch coin worth about a penny ha'penny. The car engine sounded rather rough – I'd have to have another session with it when I got home. I had my windows closed, but the smell of hot hay filtered into the car nevertheless. Even the farmers must be pleased with the weather we'd been having. The Namur motorway runs through green and pleasant countryside and it's a lovely road to drive.

My exit road was signposted to Transinne and Libin. I slowed and came off the motorway, stopped and checked my route, then proceeded, propping the map up on the dashboard. There was almost no traffic off the motorway at all. The housekeeper's instructions were exact. Who says women can't give accurate directions? After a number of right and left turns, I nosed slowly into a narrow forest road, which eventually branched into two

166

tracks. I took the left-hand one, following the map, past a sign which said *Propriété privée*. The car rolled and bumped over deep, dry ruts and fallen branches, and dust rose from the dry ground. The thickness of the trees filtered out the bright sunlight which had accompanied me all day. The forest was very beautiful, but all those thick trees clustering in on me were a rather menacing sight. I might have been at the bottom of the sea.

Then the track emerged into a small clearing, and I saw what looked like a large log cabin with a smaller one beside it and a shed a little distance away. I cut the engine, and there was silence, except for the bird-calls. I got out.

A white hatchback was parked inside the shack, but there seemed to be nobody about. I called out: 'Madame Wychell! Are you there? It's Matilda Haycastle. I'd like to talk to you.'

There was no answer. I walked up the steps to the small verandah, and as I did so, the door opened and a large, placid-looking golden retriever came out and looked at me amiably.

'Hello,' I said, going up and holding my hand out for him to sniff. He leaned against me amicably, then flopped down on the wooden floor. Pulling the door further open, I went into the cabin. It had looked rough from the outside, but now I could see that a lot of money had been spent on it. Inside was a pleasant wood-lined living room, the focus of which was a blue-and-white tiled stove set into an open fireplace. There was a big dining table with six comfortable chairs. The single window was large and double-glazed, gaily curtained. One wall had been converted into a kitchenette with cupboards, enamel sink, a small fridge and a gas cooker. A spare gas-bottle stood in one corner. The nearest town or village must be some distance away. I guessed that the place probably had its own small generator. It gets cold up here in the hunting season.

'Is there anybody there?' I called.

A door at the back of the cabin opened, and Françoise Wychell stood there, dressed in khaki skirt and shirt, sun-glasses pushed up on the top of her head. She didn't look startled. She must have heard me call the first time.

'Miss Haycastle. This is an unexpected surprise,' she said, heavily ironical. 'May I ask what you are doing here? You know that this is private land?'

'Yes, I know, and I'm very sorry to disturb you, but there was no other way to get in touch with you. There's something rather urgent I need to ask you.'

'If it's about this wretched festival of Julian's, I can't tell you anything,' she said, moving into the cabin and reaching for her cigarette case, which was on the table. 'I'm not involved in it at all. Nor am I interested.' She lit up, took a puff, and put the cigarette in the ashtray, where it smouldered gently.

'It wasn't about that,' I said. 'It's something more personal. I was talking to Isabelle Lefèvre yesterday. She told me that she's having an affair with Julian, and also that both you and he know something about Connie Trevor. She said you'd confirm it. I'm sorry, but I need to know if it's true.'

She stared at me for a long moment in amazement, and I had a moment's horrible thought. Suppose Isabelle had set me up? Suppose I'd just broken the news of a man's infidelity to his unsuspecting wife? But then she gave a short laugh like a bark, and turned to pick up the cigarette again.

'But this is perfectly extraordinary. Do you realize what you are doing? You have driven all the way here on a Sunday afternoon to ask me if my husband is having an affair with another woman? What possible business is it of yours?'

'None, I suppose,' I said. 'But I'm trying to find out what's happened to Connie and this might help. That's why I'm here, not because of Isabelle's little adventures. I couldn't care less whom she sleeps with.'

'She told you she was sleeping with Julian?'

I nodded.

'Do you believe her?' she said, her cold sea-witch's eyes on mine. It occurred to me that I wouldn't want to have Françoise Wychell as an enemy.

168

'I don't know. No, I don't think so. I can't see any sign of it in their behaviour.'

She studied me for a long moment. The door creaked open and I jumped, but it was only the dog. She put her hand down to him.

'*Viens, Jérémy*,' she said, and he trotted obediently over and rubbed his head against her skirt.

'There is no reason why I should tell you anything,' she said.

'No,' I admitted. 'There isn't.'

There was another silence. She hadn't ordered me off the premises. I waited.

'You are partly right,' Françoise said suddenly. 'I do not wish to destroy your illusions, but there was something between Isabelle and my husband, a year or two ago. She threw herself at him and he – well, he is a man, like all the others. It was over almost immediately. She is not the kind of woman who could keep Julian's attention for long. But she is a *petite hystérique névrosée* and she persists in pursuing Julian. It is most inconvenient, since we all see so much of one another socially, but there is nothing we can do. We can hardly have her locked up. She is wildly jealous of anyone to whom he pays attention. Me, my daughter, Vibeke Ferguson, you. I imagine she feels that he has been taking too much of an interest in you. May I ask in what context her remarkable revelations took place?'

'I was having lunch with your husband,' I said.

She gave another of those short, bark-like laughs.

'You see?' she said.

I saw. She gave me a look which was not without sympathy. The dog sighed and lay down heavily on the floor at her feet.

'I'm afraid your journey has been quite wasted, Miss Haycastle,' she said.

Saying I felt like a complete pill would have been a wild understatement.

'And Connie Trevor?' I asked.

'There our little Isabelle has misled you totally. Neither of us knows anything about this Connie Trevor apart from what we all learned the other night: that she was Graham's secretary and Karin Andersen's colleague and that she is unaccountably missing. I can tell you no more, and neither can Julian. Have you thought of asking Graham?'

'I don't think he's talking to me any more,' I said glumly.

'Are you satisfied? May I hope to be left in peace now?' she asked in her deep, ironical voice.

'Yes, I'll go,' I said. 'I'm sorry to have bothered you. Thank you for talking to me.'

From the way my face was feeling, I think it must have been about to go supernova. I couldn't get out of there fast enough. She came out of the cabin to watch me turn the car round, and stood there with her arms folded, smoke drifting up from the cigarette in her fingers, a half-smile on her face. I pulled laboriously out of the clearing and made my slow and dusty way back towards the main road.

Big fat zero. OK, so Julian had had a brief fling with Isabelle. It happens. Where did that leave me? It left me right back where I'd started, with Graham Ferguson. Who must have been the person that Mick Taylor had overheard quarrelling with Connie and later making up. Who must have been the 'friend' she was going to spend a week with on her return from Italy. Who was, in the delightful French phrase, *un chaud lapin* – a man who leaps on everything female in sight. Who didn't give tuppence what his wife or family thought, or, in his arrogance, believed he could keep them fooled. Who had reacted angrily when Connie's name was mentioned.

To hell with the Antwerp police. I knew I was right.

The car played up again on the way home. It was getting old. So was I, by the minute.

In my post-box when I got home was a communication from Georges, hand-delivered, hand-written (no doubt with a gold fountain pen) on Georges's expensive, embossed personal stationery. I sat down at my dining table to read it.

'*Chère Mathilde,*

Having failed to contact you by telephone despite repeated unfruitful efforts, this is to let you know that the following piece of information has floated to the surface of the European Commission's murky waters: Graham Ferguson was requested to resign from PICTS because of ungentlemanly conduct with a secretary. Make of this what you will. I am trying to discover the lady's name.

Yours eternally,

Georges'

'Hah,' I said to Hortense, who was sitting on the table. 'Was I right about Graham Ferguson, or was I right?'

Hortense must have thought I was right, for she got up, stretched, stepped down on to my lap and then jumped down to the floor before strolling off in the direction of her food dish.

I thought that maybe I should speak to Luc, but he didn't ring, and I hadn't got a number for him. I could have rung all the hotels in Antwerp but I wasn't feeling Herculean. I gave up on the world and went to bed.

The next morning didn't exactly dawn very promisingly. Well, to be truthful, I didn't see the dawn. I rose late. As I was having a rather bleary-eyed lunch, I suddenly remembered the blasted wedding present I hadn't bought. As usual I'd left it till the last minute and the wedding was in a couple of days' time. I had to move fast.

There had been no news from Antwerp. No doubt the inquisitioners were all gathered round Nigel's bedside waiting for him to recover so they could get the hot irons out again.

My friends had set up a wedding list at a big store downtown, so I had to go down to the Rue Neuve. I was just about to leave when the phone rang. Like a million people before me, I considered not answering, but didn't have the strength of mind.

'Matilda,' Georges's voice boomed down the line. 'At last. Did you see my letter?'

'Yes, thanks, Georges. And I'll bet my bottom dollar Ferguson left all his other jobs for much the same sort of reason.'

'It's possible. Do you have any news for me?'

I told him about Luc being in Antwerp, and why. He made a clucking noise with his tongue.

'A blood-stained towel is not necessarily proof of murder,' he said. 'Connie might have had an accident playing squash. That should be easy enough to find out. And why should your Nigel have killed her?'

'Exactly what I said. But Luc's got the bit between his teeth. I thought I had another lead here. That's why I was out yesterday afternoon. I'd been told something that seemed significant, so I drove down to the Wychells' cabin in the Ardennes and spoke to Françoise. But it turned out to be a red herring.'

'You spoke to Françoise?' Georges said, so abruptly that I was startled.

'Yes. Why shouldn't I?'

'Didn't you hear the news this morning?' Georges asked, every affectation gone from his voice.

'No. Why?'

'Françoise Wychell is dead. She died last night in the Ardennes.'

Chapter 21

I listened in horrified silence while Georges went on rapidly.

'It seems that there was a fire at the cabin overnight. Françoise was a heavy smoker, as you know, and the police think she left a cigarette burning in the ashtray when she went to bed. The whole area is tinder-dry, of course, after the summer we have had, and since there are no habitations nearby, it was some time before the alarm was raised. The fire-brigade was only just able to stop the fire from spreading into the adjoining forest. They think that Françoise must have been overcome by the smoke as she slept and was burned in her bed.'

'How ghastly,' I said, my throat thick. I remembered the last sight I'd had of her, wreathed in smoke on the cabin doorstep. 'Her poor family. And the poor kids, too. Where's Julian? Have they been able to get hold of him?'

'Yes, fortunately he phoned home this morning and they told him the news. He is on his way back from Germany now. You should inform the police of your visit. It may help them establish times and so on.'

'Yes, yes, you're right. I will. Thanks, Georges.'

After Georges had rung off, it took me some time to get my mind round what had happened. It's difficult to believe that a woman you've seen in perfect health the previous day is now dead. Burned alive. I shivered at the thought. I wondered what had happened to the dog. He must have been overcome by the smoke too, not to have given the alarm. Poor things.

I called the police number Luc had given me, but they

wouldn't tell me where he was and I had to be content with leaving an urgent message for him to ring me. I couldn't face explaining everything to complete strangers. Then I walked restlessly round the apartment for a while. This was awful. I'd go nuts staying in the flat all day turning the thought of Françoise over and over in my mind. I still had to get that wretched present, too. Luc would call back if he didn't get me the first time.

I went downstairs and got into the car.

It wouldn't start. Blast and damn.

I had a dig around under the bonnet, but I couldn't figure out what the trouble was. I'd have to call *Touring Secours*. But later. Time was getting on and I had to get that present. Double blast and damn. What a day this was turning out to be.

I think I dozed on the bus going downtown, which is some feat, as anyone who knows the Brussels cobblestones will tell you. It was already late afternoon, the Rue Neuve was full of people, and the store was pandemonium. I got to the wedding-list department and sat down with an elegant saleslady to choose a present. I wouldn't go for a wedding list, myself, in the unlikely event that I ever get married. I suppose it avoids the problem of getting twenty identical toasters, but it does take away the element of surprise. All the best items were already crossed off. I decided on a set of hand-embroidered table-linen. I could have had it delivered, but I decided to take it away with me and give it to my friends myself. That way they'd never know how late I'd left it. The store people did one of their fancy wrapping jobs and I set off down the crowded escalators with my plastic bags. I kept thinking about the dog.

The summer sales were in full swing on the ground floor. They have them earlier every year. I pushed my way through the crowds, got out on to the Rue Neuve, and stopped for a moment, debating whether to head for the métro at Place Rogier or Place de Brouckère.

As I stood there, a man came walking purposefully through the crowds from the direction of the Boulevard

Adolphe Max. He looked familiar. I stared. He was coming right towards me, but he wasn't looking my way. His eyes were fixed on the ground and he was frowning.

'Julian,' I said, and he looked up and saw me. He looked very tired and strained, as well he might. There were deep shadows under his eyes. He stopped abruptly and I took a step forward, concerned.

'Are you all right? Georges has told me what's happened. I know it's not much help, but I wanted to say how terribly sorry I am. Is there anything I can do to help?'

He looked at me for a moment and a faint smile broke through the tiredness on his face. 'Dear Matilda – I wouldn't have expected any less of you, but I really don't think there's anything that can be done now. Thank God, the children are at the coast with Françoise's family, so they'll be in good hands till I can get up there myself. When things like this happen, everything gets turned upside down. I haven't even had time to get home for a change of clothes. My lawyers wanted me to call in and see them immediately.' He waved a vague hand at the streets behind him.

'You should go home and have a hot bath and something to eat,' I said. Florence Nightingale rides again.

'That sounds like good advice,' he said, the tired smile still on his face. 'The police want to talk to me, too. I hope I won't have to go down to the Ardennes today.' He rubbed his face with his hands, then took a deep breath and seemed to pull himself together. 'Listen, my car's in the store car-park. Can I drop you anywhere?'

'I don't want to bother you—' I began, but he interrupted.

'No bother. I'd be glad of the company, to tell the truth. You'd be doing me a favour.'

There was no sign of the crowds thinning out in the store. We fought our way to the lift and went up to the store's multi-level car-park. Julian didn't say anything in the lift going up. Too tired probably. He must have really burned up the autobahn getting back so soon.

We emerged on to the flat roof of the car-park. He led

the way to a large gunmetal-grey BMW and felt in his pocket for the automatic gadget to open the doors. My eye was caught by a movement inside the car, and a large dog's head heaved up and greeted us with a bark. It was a golden retriever. They must have had a pair. There was a click, and the car locks sprang open.

'You can put your bags in the back,' Julian said, opening the driver's door.

'OK,' I said, and headed automatically for the boot. It swung open under my hand, and I found myself staring down at an object I recognized instantly. There, lying among a litter of rubbish, was Françoise Wychell's silver cigarette case, bullet indentations and all.

'That's funny,' I said, frowning.

'What?'

'Isn't that Françoise's cigarette case in the boot?'

There was a brief pause, and then Julian said: 'Yes. I found it under the front seat – she must have left it there when she last used the car.'

'No she didn't,' I said. 'She had it with her when I saw her in the Ardennes yesterday.'

The silence was longer this time. Then Julian appeared round the back of the car, his face expressionless. 'You saw her in the Ardennes yesterday?'

The dog barked again. Wychell said, with slight irritation: '*Tais-toi, Jérémy.*'

'I went to talk to her. I saw the cigarette case in her hand.'

'You must have been mistaken,' he said. The look on his face was watchful now.

'No I'm not. The dog was there as well.'

'We have two.'

'Both called *Jérémy?*' I asked. 'I don't think so. You're lying. You must have seen Françoise after I did.'

And then I knew why, and I suddenly felt cold. It was a wild, wild guess, but it had to be right.

I said slowly: 'You drove from Germany to the Ardennes last night, killed Françoise somehow and set fire to the cabin. Then you drove back to Germany again. But you couldn't bring yourself to leave the dog, could you?'

'Don't be utterly ridiculous,' he said angrily. 'All right, I went to the cabin and saw Françoise. So what? We needed to talk. Why on earth should I want to kill her?'

'There's a reason,' I said. 'Somewhere among all the lies you've been telling me, there's a reason.'

'Matilda, nobody's been lying to you,' he said exasperatedly. 'Maybe the shock's made me express myself badly, or maybe we're just misunderstanding one another. I haven't lied.'

'What about Connie Trevor?' I said.

He looked at me blankly for a second, then rubbed a hand over his face.

'Connie Trevor?' he said. 'For God's sake, why are you still going on about Connie Trevor? You told me yourself that she's safe and sound in California.'

I got it then. All of it. I stared at him, horrified. He looked at my face, and I recognized the expression on his. He was mentally rerunning the tapes, trying to work out what he'd said that had given me the clue.

'Isabelle was right,' I said hoarsely. I could feel my legs trembling. 'And I was right about everything except the name. It wasn't Graham at all. It was you. You were Connie's lover. You killed her. And you killed Françoise because she'd found out somehow and was threatening to expose you.'

'Absolute rubbish,' he said. 'You can't prove a word of it.'

'I didn't tell you the letter was from California,' I said. 'How could you have known unless you'd sent it yourself?'

If ever I'd needed confirmation, I saw it in his face. The tiredness dropped from it like a mask, to be replaced by anger, sharp awareness of danger and a sudden urgent purpose.

I dropped the wedding present and ran for my life.

I've always been a fast runner; having long legs helps. I belted across the flat roof of the parking area towards the ramp that led downwards to freedom, dodging the cars backing in and out of the parking slots. I heard Wychell utter a short explosive obscenity before taking off headlong after me. In my mind was the same short sentence, over and over: 'Isabelle was right. Isabelle was right.'

Luckily, I always wear sensible shoes for shopping. I hadn't run like that since I left school, but there was no time to think. I went straight for my goal, leaping obstacles like a chamois: low walls, ventilation domes, people's shopping. My foot scattered a stack of bags waiting to be loaded into a car. The ramp entrance loomed up and I plunged down into the gloom, Wychell hard behind me.

I remember thinking that it was a ludicrously dangerous thing to do. The car-park was four storeys high and the spiral access ramp was narrow, tight and dark. The concrete floor was slippery and steep. I felt my soles skid, and threw out my arms to steady myself. The yellow line in the middle of the ramp wound downwards and I pounded down it, panting.

As I reached the second floor, packed with parked cars, I heard the sudden screech of tyres down below and saw headlights swing wildly across the wall in the next stretch of tunnel. There's always some smart-ass who comes roaring up at eighty just for the hell of it. I barely had time to throw myself clear before the car hurtled thunderously round the corner. Wychell, still in the tunnel behind me, had no escape. As I fell heavily against a parked car and bounced off on to the cement floor, I heard a shout, a soggy thump and then the solid, unmistakable crash of metal against concrete and the tinkle of broken glass.

There was a short interval of silence before the fuss started. I didn't feel like moving, so I didn't. My knee felt mashed. It hurt. I wondered if Wychell was dead. Somebody bent over me and asked if I was all right. Damn fool question. An ambulance arrived, followed by a police car. You'd have thought they'd switch their sirens off in a multi-storey car-park. A shocked young man, covered in blood, was explaining at the top of his voice over and over again how it had happened. After a while, I stopped listening.

Chapter 22

Wychell wasn't dead, but he wasn't going anywhere for a while. A long while, if I had anything to do with it. The police interviewed me in the hospital casualty department, while a silent young black doctor carefully dressed my cuts and bruises and bound up my knee.

The story sounded fantastic even to me. The police didn't know what I was talking about at first. They looked at one another perplexedly and talked about concussion. Then, by some blessed inspiration, I got them to ring Georges, who came straight down to the hospital. After that things started to happen. Some rather senior police officers appeared and took a long statement from me. A distressed overweight Belgian, who turned out to be Françoise's brother, came down and identified the ciga- rette case and confirmed that the Wychells only had one dog. A forensic team was dispatched immediately by heli- copter to the Ardennes, with instructions to search the scene of the fire minutely. Luc was summoned from Antwerp and appeared in such a short time that he must have come by Concorde. I sat on my trolley in casualty, surrounded by people, like Louis XIV at his *levée*.

By that stage, I just wanted to go home. They let me, finally. Georges and Luc had a brief argument about who was going to drive me home, and Georges won, by dint of having a more comfortable car.

'Of course, it's obvious to any Belgian why Julian would have wished to do away with Françoise,' Georges said, fussily arranging cushions around me. 'From what Mel- chior de Jonckheere was just telling me, the Wychells'

180

marriage contract prevented him from getting a penny without his wife's approval.'

'Which she only gave as long as he was discreet,' I said. 'And which no doubt she would have withdrawn at the slightest suspicion of implication in Connie Trevor's disappearance.'

'*Juste*,' Georges said, with a nod. 'Melchior told me that Wychell wanted more money to expand the business into Eastern Europe, but the family had refused.'

'And the only way to get his hands on the spondulicks would be if Françoise died,' I said. 'So he had a double motive. And that explains why the first thing he did was go to his lawyers. And if he hadn't, he'd never have met me by accident and I'd never have twigged.'

'All we need now,' Georges said, 'are the bodies.'

He tapped on the glass partition between us and Albert. The Bentley glided smoothly away from the kerb. Behind us, Luc pulled away in his car, somewhat less smoothly.

Luckily, the police got it right this time. It took them a few days, mind you. They sifted through the ashes and didn't find a whole lot there, but when they went over the area with tracker dogs and iron detectors and the works, they found something much more important, as far as I was concerned. They found Connie, buried in the forest not far from the cabin.

I knew it was Connie straight away, though the police waited till the dental records had been checked before they'd commit themselves. After all, who else could it be? She'd died from a fractured skull. She'd also been four months pregnant. And after that, everybody started to sing like little yellow birds.

'Matilda heard such dreadful lies'. Sorry, Mr Belloc, but it would have been much more appropriate. I was chastened to learn how many lies I'd swallowed. And I hadn't believed Isabelle, because she was the last person I'd expected to be telling the truth.

Ferguson couldn't tell the police enough. As I'd surmised, he was a twenty-fingered toucher-up, and he'd had a go at Connie when she was his secretary at PICTS. Connie had not only made an official complaint, but when her contract wasn't renewed, she had brought an action for unfair dismissal as well. Ferguson offered her money to drop the case but Connie, typically, had her mind made up.

According to Ferguson, it was Wychell who had the bright idea of seeing whether charm would work where money had failed. It did. Connie, the arch-romantic, had met the love of her life. Wychell had no difficulty persuading her to drop both complaints, on the pretext that Ferguson was now his partner and the publicity would harm him too. He got her the job at Sundsvall and the affair had gone on ever since. In parallel, as it happened, with his affair with Isabelle. The contrast between them must have amused him.

No wonder Ferguson had been so jumpy every time Connie's name was mentioned, with all that on his conscience. Not to mention the fact that Vibeke didn't know about the sexual harassment or indeed anything else.

Nice people I'd been going round with.

Isabelle, enjoying every minute in the limelight, gave them all the juicy details about Wychell's affairs; and faced with the evidence, Wychell himself told the police the rest. He'd promised to marry Connie and she was becoming more and more insistent that he keep his promise. Finally, she threatened to make the affair public. And then, just before the Italian holiday, she told him she was pregnant. I remembered the pack of unopened pills I'd found in her bathroom all those weeks ago. Well, it's a tried and tested way of pushing a dithering man into commitment, and we all know people who've done it. But Connie had picked the wrong man. They quarrelled. Wychell broke it off. Then he had a change of heart. Or more likely, I said to myself cynically, he suddenly got scared that Connie might sell the story to the *News of the World*. It has, after all, been done before. So he invited her to his Brussels *pied-à-terre* after her Italian holiday, hoping to settle the affair amicably. She arrived direct from the station with her suitcase. He offered her money for an abortion. She became hysterical, and he lost his temper and struck out. According to Wychell, Connie fell and hit her head on the corner of the sideboard. Well, maybe she did.

I wondered how he'd felt when he saw she was dead. Remorse? Probably not. The first thought must have been a practical one. What do you do with a dead body?

He waited till dark, took Connie down in the lift to the underground car-park, put her in the boot of his car, drove to the Ardennes and buried her on his wife's private land. A neat touch. He emptied the suitcase and put handbag and clothes into a collecting bin for Third World countries. They were probably on their way to Afghanistan by now. The suitcase was dumped in a skip in another part of town. He destroyed all her personal belongings. All except one. In her handbag was an unposted letter to Linda. This was an unexpected find. He typed a new note, copied the signature, put the whole thing back in the genuine envelope, sent it to a US business contact and asked him to post it. It was, he said, for a child who collected foreign stamps.

He might have got away with it. Connie had no close family ties and few real friends. People come and go so much in Brussels that her disappearance would hardly have been noticed. The Sundsvall people might have made enquiries, but Wychell knew enough about the situation in the office to realize that any interest would have been half-hearted. Connie's bank would have kept on paying mortgage, electricity, gas and telephone bills regularly till the money ran out, by which time the trail would have been long cold. And what was one more missing person in the vast immensity of the United States?

His only miscalculation was Hortense. He probably didn't even know that Connie had a cat. And if it hadn't been for Hortense, I'd never have got involved. It must have been a real shock when I turned up and Karin dropped me right in it. But he was a clever man. He'd led me up the garden path with consummate expertise. It embarrassed me to think about it.

Françoise had been playing her own games. She'd

known about Connie, of course. She'd lied blind to me at the cabin. She'd put up with Wychell's affairs for years. Divorcing him for adultery was unthinkable. She had the family, her children, her social position to think of. Then my enquiries made her suspect that her husband knew more than he was telling about Connie's disappearance. Here was a possible way to force him into a quiet, discreet divorce by mutual consent, with no stain on the family escutcheon. What she actually did was sign the order for her own execution. Wychell had to move fast. The trip to Germany was a good alibi. The kids were at the coast. Françoise was alone in a deserted spot. It must have seemed perfect. A touch of chloroform, and a good blaze to destroy all the evidence. But he'd forgotten about the dog. He was fond of the dog. And in the hurry to get away, he didn't remember till later that he'd shoved the cigarette case into his pocket instead of leaving it on the scene, as he'd intended.

So there it was. Kisses and flowers for me, and leg-irons for Wychell. If Françoise's family had anything to do with it, they'd put him in the deepest oubliette in Bouillon Castle and throw away the key.

Poor old Nigel Grant had been telling the truth too. Luc's blood-stained towel turned out, as Georges had predicted, to be the result of a nosebleed on the squash-court just before Connie's holiday. I felt I owed Nigel one, so I persuaded Georges to pull a string or two. The Antwerp police shrugged their shoulders, waited till Nigel was on his feet again, took him to Ostend and put him on the boat for Dover. I hoped the lesson had been a salutary one, but I doubted it. My conscience, however, felt clearer.

De Jonckheere, Ferguson and Wychell was wrapped up overnight, and not long afterwards, I heard that Vibeke had left her husband and returned to Sweden with her children. I had liked Vibeke. Then, after the police formalities were over, Linda and David flew over to deal with Connie's affairs and to take her back home, to be buried beside her parents. Linda was as pleasant as she'd sounded on the phone, but Connie'd been right about David. He was a wimp. He was, however, efficient. I watched, somewhat disheartened, as they dismantled the left-overs of Connie's life. The furniture and car were sold off and the apartment put up for sale. In the end, all that was left was Hortense. I asked if I could keep her and Linda gratefully said 'Yes'. Then they took Connie home, at last.

There was a lot of unwelcome publicity, of course. The local English language press had some real news to report for once and they made the most of it. People kept ringing up to get the story, but I wasn't allowed to tell them anything.

All I wanted to do was get out of town. I finally got the car repaired, and Luc and I headed for the Midi, leaving Hortense to the tender ministrations of Georges, who has an incongruous passion for 'les p'tites mimines'. It was raining when we left Brussels, but south of the Loire the sun came out again and that's the way it was for the whole three weeks.

It was the nearest thing to a honeymoon that I'll probably ever have, staying in small hotels, sleeping in beds of all shapes and sizes, eating wondrous meals in tiny country villages. We explored castles and vineyards, searched for forgotten Roman ruins in the sun-drenched fields, went to *son-et-lumière* shows and to concerts in ancient little churches. Neither of us had had a proper holiday for years. We were amazingly happy, although we knew that things probably wouldn't be easy when we got home. But we didn't let the thought bother us too much.